An Almost Perfect Game

Other books by Stephen Manes

Comedy High
Chocolate-Covered Ants
Make Four Million Dollars by Next Thursday!
Be a Perfect Person in Just Three Days!
Chicken Trek
The Obnoxious Jerks
It's New! It's Improved! It's Terrible!
Some of the Adventures of Rhode Island Red
Monstra vs. Irving
The Great Gerbil Roundup
The Oscar J. Noodleman Television Network
That Game from Outer Space
Video War
Life Is No Fair!
The Hooples' Horrible Holiday
The Hooples' Haunted House
Slim Down Camp
Socko! Every Riddle Your Feet Will Ever Need
Pictures of Motion and Pictures that Move
The Boy Who Turned into a TV Set
I'll Live
Hooples on the Highway
Mule in the Mail
The Complete MCI Mail Handbook

With Esther Manes:
The Bananas Move to the Ceiling

With Paul Andrews:
Gates: How Microsoft's Mogul Reinvented an Industry — and Made Himself the Richest Man in America

An Almost Perfect Game

STEPHEN MANES

SCHOLASTIC
HARDCOVER

Scholastic Inc.
New York

Library of Congress Cataloging-in-Publication Data

Manes, Stephen, 1949–
An almost perfect game / Stephen Manes.
p.   cm.
Summary: As he and his grandmother keep score at the last
game of the season for the local minor league team,
Jake and his older brother begin to wonder if
Jake's scorecard can control the outcome of the game.
ISBN 0-590-44432-8
[1. Baseball — Fiction. 2. Brothers — Fiction.
3. Grandparents — Fiction.]
I. Title.
PZ7.M31264An   1995
[Fic] — dc20   94-18192
                                                        CIP
                                                         AC

12 11 10 9 8 7 6 5 4 3 2 1   5 6 7 8 9/9 0/0

Designed by Ursula Herzog

Printed in the U.S.A.   37

First printing, May 1995

for Grandma and Gramps

An Almost Perfect Game

Warmup

K.

The letter *K.*

I don't want to sound like *Sesame Street* or something, but the letter *K* is what started the whole thing. You know, *K*? The letter between *J* and *L*?

I guess I *am* sounding like *Sesame Street*. The point is that if I had written *J*, the whole thing probably never would have happened. *J* doesn't mean much of anything in baseball. *K* means strikeout.

And when I accidentally wrote the letter *K* in my scorecard beside the name of Duke Mountain, right fielder for the Nottingham Shoppers, here's what happened next:

Strike one!
Strike two!
Strike three!

Top of
the First

It was the last game of the year for the Shoppers. Warming up on the mound: our most experienced pitcher, a pudgy blond left-handed junkballer named Dirk Wade. Some people called him "Jerk" Wade, but he was my favorite guy on the team. Part of it was that even though he was kind of pockmarked and weathered and gnarly he still looked kind of handsome, which made me feel a little better about my pimples. He also had a beer gut, which made me feel a little better about my personal roundness.

I especially liked him because he was so cool about autographs. After a game, Wade would autograph just about anything you tossed his way. Anything. I had Dirk Wade autographed baseball cards, Dirk Wade autographed baseballs, a Dirk Wade autographed glove, a Dirk Wade autographed bat, and a Dirk Wade autographed book bag. I also had a Dirk Wade

autographed hockey puck, a Dirk Wade autographed basketball, and Dirk Wade autographed
underpants, all of which I got after dares from
my brother, Randy.

Randy said Wade was a "signing fool" because
he was a lot older than most of the guys on the
team, so he was too old to be snotty. He had
pitched in the low minors and even three innings
in triple-A before he blew out his arm and needed
surgery. The local paper said he was trying to
make a comeback after five years away from the
game. I couldn't figure out how you could make
a comeback when you were never that great in
the first place. Still, he was an okay junkball
pitcher. Even though he had an earned run average of 5.95, his record was 5 wins and 4 losses.
The Shoppers always seemed to get a lot of runs
when Wade was on the mound.

The reason some people called him "Jerk" was
that he had a lot of odd habits and superstitions.
Most of them showed up at the start of the inning. When he arrived on the mound, he always
picked up the rosin bag and juggled it a little.
Next he went to the back of the mound, faced
second base, and talked to himself for a few seconds. Then he patted himself on the butt with
his glove and took his warmups. When he was

done, he always bowed to the umpire. According to the local paper, he said, "If you're nice to them, maybe they'll be nice to you."

So now he made a low bow to the ump, and Reynaldo Ruidoso, the Wakena Apples second baseman and leadoff hitter, stepped into the batter's box. From where we sat, three rows in back of the home dugout, Ruidoso looked kind of skinny, but through my grandfather's binoculars you could see his forearms were all muscle.

Wade made a face, stepped off the mound, kicked the dirt around, and talked to himself again. Sometimes it took him a while to get comfortable out there.

The crowd was still settling down, too. Tonight was the last game of the regular season, and the park was mobbed. For one thing, this was Fan Appreciation Night, when the team gave away a whole mess of free prizes. But there was another reason why so many fans were crowding in: Wakena and Nottingham were tied for the lead of the Northern Division. Whoever won this game would go on to the Cascade League playoffs.

Usually we arrived in time to check out fielding practice. Tonight it took us ten minutes short of forever to park, and there was a big jam where they take the tickets to get in. Normally we all went to the concession stands together, but now we were so late that Grandma and I let Gramps and my big brother, Randy, make the food run.

It was only fair, because Randy and Gramps don't keep score. I keep score of every game I go to, and I am pretty serious about it. Grandma is even more serious about keeping score than I am. In fact, she's the one who taught me how to do it.

And tonight I was lucky even to get a score-card. When Grandma and I stepped up to the program vendor, he was shouting, "Lucky program scorecard! Guaranteed lucky!"

It was the same guy I always bought my program from, a short fellow with a dark beard and sunglasses beneath his Shoppers cap. Usually he had a whole stack of programs, but with the crowd tonight, he looked like he was down to his very last one. "What do you mean, guaranteed lucky?" I asked him.

"First off, here's Dirk Wade's autograph." He opened it to the inside of the front cover, where there was a photo of all the Shoppers.

"Why did he sign this?" I asked suspiciously.

"Hey, he always signs one. It's part of his routine. Like that little dance he does when he crosses the foul line between innings. He says it brings him luck."

"He needs it, with that earned run average," I said.

"You got that right," the vendor agreed.

"So what's this about guaranteed lucky?"

"Lucky for him, I hope. Lucky for you, guaranteed. If you don't win a prize tonight, I give you a free scorecard tomorrow."

"Some guarantee! There won't *be* a tomorrow if the Shoppers don't win tonight."

"What kind of fan are you? You're not an Apples fan!"

"Of course not!" I pointed to my Shoppers cap.

"Well, of course we'll win! You want this or don't you?"

I forked over a dollar. "Remember," he said. "Guaranteed lucky."

Yeah. Maybe. Another one of Dirk Wade's goofy superstitions.

Slow curve, low and away. Ball one on Ruidoso. Randy and my grandfather arrived at our seats with armloads of hot dogs and nachos and pizza and a big plastic-bagged stalk of the cotton candy none of us liked but Grandma.

"Sorry it took us so long," Gramps said.

"Too bad you missed 'The Star-Spangled Banner,' " Grandma told him. "A cute little girl from Plank School sang it."

"Cute, but her voice stank," I said.

6

"Jake!" Grandma scolded.

Fast ball on the outside corner. Strike one called.

"We heard it over the loudspeakers," Gramps said. "I think Jake has a point."

Randy nodded and held his nose. "You should've seen the lines out there! Halfway to the Canadian border!"

"Fan Appreciation Night," Grandma said. "Always a full house."

Ruidoso danced away from an inside fast ball and gave Wade a dirty look.

"Fan Appreciation Night, Opening Night, and Rooster Night," Gramps said. "Three biggest crowds of the year."

Big swing, strike two. Ruidoso choked up on the bat a little.

"Is this guy a Star of the Future?" Randy asked me as he unwrapped a hot dog. It was a joke we had between us. A huge sign outside the park read HAROLD ERRICHETTI MEMORIAL STADIUM: WHERE THE STARS OF THE FUTURE SHINE. We had been coming here five years, and so far only a couple of the guys we had seen had made it to the majors, mostly for a few at bats in September. Nobody in his right mind would call them stars.

"What do you say?" Randy demanded.

7

"I say where's my hot dog of the present? And my nachos?"

"Poor starving child," he teased. "Some scout you are."

I made a face at him. "I need food, not sarcasm."

The crowd roared. I looked back toward the plate. The batter muttered something he shouldn't've and headed for the dugout. "Strikeout?" I asked.

"You can't keep the score if you don't watch the game," Grandma scolded. She scowled as I snuck a peek at her scorebook and the *K* for called strikeout in Ruidoso's frame for the first inning. She didn't like me to look over and read her scorekeeping and fix mine up to match hers. She considered it kind of like cheating.

"I'll catch up in a second," I promised. "Just let me get some nourishment."

"Strike out the first batter, you lose the game," Randy said.

"One of those old baseball superstitions," Gramps muttered.

"I bet Wade believes it," I said.

"He believes every one there is," Randy agreed. "Look at him out there, talking to himself."

"Not a stitch of truth in any of 'em," Gramps said. "Except one."

"Which one's that?" I asked.

"The team that scores the most runs in a game always wins," Grandma and Gramps said at the same time.

Grandma smiled. "When you live with somebody as long as I have, you know most of his jokes by heart." Gramps reached around to Grandma and gave her a little squeeze.

"Now batting, number nine, Wakena left fielder, Ben Covington." I looked toward the plate. A wiry black guy stepped up and kicked the back line of the batter's box around until you couldn't see it anymore.

Gramps looked down at a row of hot dogs in a gray cardboard box that was turning kind of soggy on his lap. "What's on yours again?"

"As if you didn't know!" In my family I was notorious for my hot dogs.

"Aha! Ketchup, mustard, relish, onions, sauerkraut, jalapeños. Here you go." Gramps handed me a bed of napkins with my beautiful, dripping, oozing, gook-overflowing hot dog on top. My grandfather was almost as good at adding the fixings to hot dogs as I was. He had taught me his condiment secrets, but I'd added a few improvements of my own.

"See if you can keep most of it off your shirt," my grandmother said. It wouldn't have mattered

9

anyway. Most of my T-shirts are decorated with food souvenirs. There's a mustard stain here, a ketchup stain there. I even have root beer stains on a couple of my shoes.

My brother passed me a paper basket of nachos smothered in jalapeños, the way I liked them. "Just don't sit anywhere near me for the next three days," he said, holding his nose and squinching up his face. "Your breath could melt the paint off the dugout from here."

I managed to balance the hot dog on my left knee and the nachos on my right knee, and then Grandma handed me my super-enormous root beer. Keeping score and eating dinner at the same time wasn't going to be easy.

As I passed the binoculars back to Gramps, I heard the crack of the bat. I turned to see the shortstop grab a slow roller and nail Covington at first. Grandma took a bite of her hot dog and wrote 6–3 in the next box of the scorebook. "Now you're two plays behind," she said.

I wasn't worried. I could handle it. I took a big bite of my hot dog and washed it down with a swig of root beer. Wakena's huge first baseman, Fred Pelc, lumbered up to the plate.

Pelc was supposed to be a genuine Star of the Future, because he'd had a great career in some college down in California. He was a first-round draft pick, and he'd signed for a lot of money, but so far he had mostly hit a lot of long outs.

The local paper said he was still uncomfortable with wooden bats after using aluminum ones for so many years. When my grandfather read that, he snorted, "No wonder! Aluminum bats aren't baseball!" He feels the same way about artificial turf and the designated hitter.

I put my scorecard under my arm and tried to balance the nachos and hot dog in my lap while I set the root beer between my feet. "How does the official scorekeeper do it?" I sighed.

"Don't you remember? We took you up there a couple of years ago." Grandma pointed to the press box up above the stands behind home plate.

Actually I did remember. The scorer and the announcer and the reporters sat behind long, deep tables with plenty of room for goodies. "Oh, yeah," I said as Pelc took a fast ball for a strike. "So how do *you* do it?"

Grandma wasn't quite as big a mustard and jalapeño fan as I was, but even so, her scorecards were always incredibly neat, with never so much as a stain on them. One of her goals was what she called a perfect game. This was not the same as a game where the pitcher doesn't let even one batter get on base. What Grandma meant was a game where she would get every play marked down perfectly — not a single box erased, not a single cross-out, not even a smudge. In years and years of ball games she had never quite managed it.

Her scorecards might not have been perfect, but they sure were a whole lot neater than mine. "It's all just being careful," she said.

Ball one on Pelc. "And not being," Randy grunted through an enormous mouthful of pizza, "a pig."

Grandma and I ignored him. "I'll catch up at the end of the inning," I told her. "I promise. Usually we're already done eating by now."

Grandma took another neat nibble of her hot dog and frowned.

I smiled back. "I'll score it an assist for you."

Gramps leaned across Randy and Grandma and tapped me on the shoulder. "You're just lucky, my friend, that you have a grandmother who's the greatest scorekeeper in the history of the game. Can I have some of those nachos? Whoa! Heads up!"

The "whoa!" was for a foul ball that screamed past the people sitting in the next box. "Nearly had it," Randy joked, pounding his glove. A

12

scramble broke out two aisles over. A barrel-chested guy in a T-shirt with a beer label on it came up grinning with the ball. A few people behind him applauded.

"I got it!" Gramps shouted, making a long reach into my nacho basket, pulling out a gooey mess, and somehow not dripping it on Randy or Grandma.

Pelc stepped back into the box and whipped the bat around like some caveman's club. Dirk Wade nodded at the catcher's sign, wound, threw. The ball sailed over the heads of the batter, the catcher, and the umpire. It got stuck so high in the screen behind home plate that the batboy had to climb up to get it. "Strike three!" bellowed a huge woman a couple of rows behind us. Everybody laughed.

Including me. Baseball: I love it. Fans relaxing, hollering, making weird jokes. Smell of hot dogs and nachos and stale beer. Sun going down behind the stands in left. Green green grass everywhere but the infield and the places where it's kind of worn out and brown this late in the season. Players in the dugout joking around but trying to look cool.

And then the windup. The pitch. The swing. The crack of the bat.

High fly ball down the right-field line. You

13

could tell by the way Duke Mountain was loping that he'd have no problem with this one. Easy out. Three up. Three down. Dirk Wade made his funny little crow-hop as he crossed the foul line on his way to the dugout.

On the scoreboard for the visitors: a big fat goose egg. Just the way we wanted it.

		R	H	E
Visitors	0	0	0	0
Shoppers				

Bottom of
the First

"Ladies and gentlemen, boys and girls," said the announcer as I swallowed my last bite of hot dog and the umpire dusted off the plate, "be sure to visit our better-than-ever Nottingham Shoppers souvenir spots, located under the stands behind first and third. Tonight's your last chance to check out the great new assortment of official Nottingham Shoppers logo souvenirs for your collection. It's the best way to show you're a — "

"Shopper Bopper!" Randy and I cried in unison, trying to imitate the announcer's voice. Somehow it's so corny it always cracks us up.

"And now, Shoppers fans, it's time for the first lucky Fan Appreciation Night number, which you'll find right below the Dan's Markets advertisement on page twenty-six of your Shoppers program. The winner will receive a one hundred dollar shopping spree at the Market of the Stars of the Future. That's Dan's! Now that lucky Fan

Appreciation Night number: three five eight nine six. Remember, all prizes must be collected before the beginning of the ninth inning."

"Win anything?" my brother asked sarcastically.

I wasn't exactly hopeful. I never won anything. We never even sat near anybody who won anything. But who knew? Tonight might be different. This program was "guaranteed lucky," wasn't it?

I checked page 26. My number was 72483. It was only something like 37000 away from a winner. Some luck! *Bad* luck. "Hooray!" I shouted.

"Yeah, right," Randy snorted.

"It says right here: a chance to dump twenty gallons of stinky fish oil on any brother of yours. What a consolation prize!"

"Very funny," said Randy. "Especially coming from Mr. Mustardface. What a gross-out!"

I looked at my grandmother. She shook her head and pointed to three places on her face, meaning that's where the mustard was on mine.

"By the way, are you going to keep score," she inquired as she handed me a bunch of napkins, "or are you just going to let me do it?"

"I'm just going to let you do it," I teased as I wiped my face.

16

Grandma pointed to a spot on my chin I had missed. "That's what it looks like."

"I'm kidding. Come on. Can I copy your first inning?"

She shook her head. "That's not much of a way to end the season." She flipped her scorebook over to the Shoppers side so I couldn't see what the Apples had done.

"I can do it off the top of my head," I bragged. I had filled in the names and numbers of the batters when they'd announced the lineups before the game, so hey, nothing to it. "First batter struck out, called third strike." And in the first box in the first inning I put the letter *K*.

That was the *K* I mentioned before. That was the *K* that started the whole thing off. That was the *K* that — well, as Grandma said, "Wrong team, smarty-pants."

I looked down. What an idiot! I had my scorecard flipped to our team's side. So instead of putting the *K* beside Reynaldo Ruidoso, leadoff hitter for the Wakena Apples, I had made a serious mistaKe.

According to my scorecard, Duke Mountain, leadoff batter for our Nottingham Shoppers, had struck out. But in real life he was out there taking practice swings in the on-deck circle while the

Apples pitcher finished his warmups. My perfect game was over before the first inning had ended.

"See what I always say about concentration?" Grandma shook her head. "No big deal. Just erase it."

"In a minute," I grumbled, mad at myself for such a stupid bush-league error. "I want to get the top of the first straightened out before I forget."

I flipped the scorecard over to the Apples side. At least I didn't have to peek at Grandma's scorebook. Ruidoso, struck out: *K.* Covington, ground out to short: *6–3.* Pelc, flied out to right: *9.* Just call me Mr. Memory.

I flipped the scorecard back to the Shoppers side. Up at the plate, Duke Mountain took a huge swing that missed the ball by a foot. Strike one.

"Close, Duke, close!" Randy shouted. Duke Mountain was his favorite Shopper. Mountain was the kind of guy who would run into the outfield wall chasing down fly balls, and he had a lot of hustle on the base paths. That name of his didn't hurt, either. Randy called him "Mountain Man" and "Man Mountain" and "The Human Volcano."

I flipped my pencil over to erase the stupid *K* in the box next to Mountain's name. Then I thought: What's the hurry? He's already got one strike. Maybe he'll strike out looking, K all over again, and my scorecard will be perfect after all.

Mountain took a pitch low and inside. One and one. Another big swing made it strike two.

"Hey, we don't need a breeze!" shouted somebody behind us. "*Hit* that ball!"

Grandma pointed to that K I had already given the batter. "Maybe you won't need to erase that after all."

Mountain fouled one off.

"Never know," I said. But I did know. At that moment I was positive that Duke Mountain was going to strike out.

And then we all knew. The ball whizzed right across the heart of the plate about knee-high. Mountain thought it was low and sat there with the bat on his shoulder. The umpire bellowed and stuck out his right arm. Mountain shook his head, softly said a dirty word, and stomped back to the dugout.

"You're a bum, Mountain!" bellowed a guy in the stands behind me.

I didn't even have to look back. It was a skinny guy with thick glasses who looked about my dad's age. He had been coming to all the games for as long as I could remember and always wore a cap that read DUMB BOZO. Every time somebody on our team struck out, this guy shouted, "You're a bum!"

My grandmother tapped her finger on my scorecard. "Well, you got lucky with that one!"

I smiled and shrugged. I didn't say what I really felt. No, not felt — *knew*. Just as sure as I had known that Duke Mountain was going to strike out, I was positive that the *K* I had written down was what had made him do it.

I guess I should explain a couple of things. My grandparents are super baseball fans. A few years ago they actually drove around the country to see a game in every major-league ballpark, and also a lot of minor-league ones. When they were younger, they even got to some parks that don't exist anymore, like the Polo Grounds in New York and Ebbets Field in Brooklyn and Connie Mack Stadium in Philadelphia. And especially Forbes Field in Pittsburgh.

Grandma and Gramps used to live in Pittsburgh, and they love to tell stories about who they saw at Forbes Field. They actually saw, in person, some of the all-time great players — Hall of Famers like Henry Aaron and Willie Mays and Sandy Koufax and Bob Gibson — and they can just about talk your ear off when it comes to

Roberto Clemente. This was back before anybody had even thought of aluminum bats or the designated hitter or artificial turf, which gives you some idea of how ancient my grandparents are.

Nowadays they live in Nottingham, Washington, which is near the Canadian border. The Nottingham team is in the Cascade League, which is a short-season class-A minor league, which means it only plays from June till Labor Day. The team is called the Nottingham Shoppers because it's owned by a guy who owns a big shopping mall where a lot of Canadians come down to buy stuff at prices cheaper than in Canada.

The team symbol is a green baseball with a silver shopping cart on it, and if you look at the baseball's seams, they sort of form a dollar sign. A lot of people think it's a stupid name and a stupider symbol, but the Shoppers used to be called the Redskins, and the owner told the local paper that a lot of Indians in the area thought that name was even stupider. He said if people didn't quit complaining, he'd change the team name to the Palefaces. People quit complaining.

Every year for as long as I can remember, my brother and I have visited my grandparents for a couple of weeks in the summer. My parents always go on a trip on their own, just the two of

21

them — "to get away from you two monsters" is what they always say, meaning me and my brother.

"Same to you and Merry Christmas," Randy always says back, and I do, too. Actually, we don't mind at all, because Grandma is a great cook, and Gramps loves to take us fishing, and we go to ball games every night the Shoppers are at home. But this year was a little different, because this year my parents were attending some special conference in France, so my brother and I spent the end of the summer in Nottingham instead of the middle. What that meant was that for a change we found ourselves in the heat of a pennant race.

At the beginning of every game I would buy a program, so I could read up on the stats and check out the uniform numbers and get those not-so-lucky "lucky" numbers that never won me a thing. And, of course, to keep score in the scorecard in the middle.

My grandmother never bought a scorecard, because she used a scorebook, the kind the official scorekeepers use in the press box, only smaller, since she liked the size that fit in her purse. My brother never bought a scorecard, because he said keeping score was the stupidest thing he'd ever heard of, and besides, he could always mooch off Grandma and me if he forgot what was happening in the game. As for my grandfather, he said he was too busy shelling peanuts to worry about keeping score.

And I know it sounds stupid, but here's what I was thinking as I watched Tony Faria, the Shoppers first baseman, walk in from the on-deck circle: I was thinking, kind of half-jokingly, that maybe this scorecard of mine did have some sort of luck in it. Or magic. I mean, look what happened with Duke Mountain: I put down a *K*, and a K it was.

Faria dug in. He was a huge right-handed batter. In the last couple of weeks we had seen him hit two or three monster home runs and at least half a dozen shots that had just missed.

"Love the way he twirls the bat kind of helicopterlike, the way Wilver Stargell did," Gramps muttered. "Except Stargell was a lefty."

"Seems to me you mentioned that once before," Grandma said.

"Maybe I did," Gramps said with a smile. "Maybe I did." Actually, he said this just about every time Faria came to bat. Stargell was one of their favorite old-time Pirates. He's in the Hall of Fame, too.

The pitcher wound and threw. A loud pop in the catcher's mitt: ball one. Our seats were just

23

three rows in back of the Shoppers dugout, so close that we could hear all kinds of interesting things — like the swearwords the batters would say when they struck out, or the way Ray Weingartner, our first-base coach, would yell, "That's the eye, that's the eye! Wait him out, wait him out!" in that singsongy voice you hear on baseball fields from tee-ball to the big leagues.

And while the pitcher stared in for his sign, I decided it was time to find out about this luck stuff. I checked the stat sheet. Faria hadn't hit a triple all season. Kind of hiding it from my grandmother — I somehow figured she wouldn't approve — I drew three-quarters of a little diamond in Tony Faria's first-inning box. In the upper-left-hand corner I put down 7 for left field. Triple to left? We'd see soon enough.

I looked up just in time to see Faria take a humongous swing at the ball. He missed it by at least two feet.

Not exactly a triple. "Wait 'im out!" somebody hollered behind me.

"Don't be a bum, Faria!" yelled a familiar voice.

Faria stepped out of the batter's box, picked up some dirt, and rubbed it on his hands. He stepped back in. The pitcher threw a slow curve. It was just hanging there . . .

Now!

There was a loud crack. Faria got all of it. My heart got this weird heavy feeling: home run. Not a triple. Some magic!

The crowd screamed every inch of the way as the ball soared in the air toward the left-field fence. Then it went over — left of the foul pole by maybe a foot. Strike two.

"Close only counts in horseshoes," Randy said.

"And shaving," my grandfather added. It was one of their running jokes.

I slid my hand over the triple in my scorecard so that Grandma couldn't see it. I was beginning to feel pretty stupid about this idea. I mean, come on. A magic scorecard? Get real. Get the eraser.

Faria took ball two, low, and then ball three, way outside. A lot of times in the minors, the pitching isn't all that great. The Apples pitcher was a left-hander named Trent Tollefson. He seemed to have a lot of heat, but not much control. According to the stats, he walked twice as many batters as he struck out. He also had an earned run average of 6.27. As Randy said, "That's why he's here instead of the majors."

Full count. Faria fouled one into the screen. Then he stepped into the box again and twirled his bat. "Make him throw strikes!" somebody shouted.

The pitcher did throw a strike. He threw it right down the heart of the plate — right in Faria's power zone. And this time Tony Faria drilled a rising line drive. "Fro! Zen! Rope!" my brother screamed.

All the Apples left fielder could do was run back hard and try to catch up. The ball bounced off the wall — actually, off the bald head of a cartoon of a chubby car dealer named Pudge Dinsmore. Then it took a weird hop toward the visitors' bull pen in left.

The crowd rose to its feet and whooped and hollered as Faria rounded first and pumped for second. The left fielder changed directions and chased after the ball. The third-base coach was waving his arm like a windmill — or Faria's bat. Tony was a power hitter, not a speedster, but he churned for third with everything he had.

The left fielder picked up the ball and fired it toward third. Faria dived headfirst into the bag. All I could see from our seats was a cloud of dust.

And then the umpire's sign: safe!

Faria called for time, got up and dusted himself off. And when I lifted my elbow from my score-card, I didn't have to write down a thing. Tony Faria's triple to left stared back at me from the page.

I pretended to mark the triple in the book even

though it was already there. I didn't want Grandma to see what I'd been doing. If she did, I'd have to explain it to her, and right now I couldn't even explain it to myself. Maybe it was just another lucky coincidence. Maybe I was just imagining that here in the stands, with my pencil and my scorecard, I could somehow control what happened out there on the field.

"Hey! You want some or don't you?" My brother was waving a bag of peanuts under my nose, and I was thinking so hard I hadn't even noticed. I shook my head and waved him away. I still had plenty of nachos left, and right now I was worrying more about my scorecard than my stomach.

"Hey, be sure to mark this in your scorecard," Randy said as he withdrew the bag.

"Mark what in?" I asked suspiciously.

"New record. First time in history Jake Kratzer has ever refused food," Randy said. "Come on. Mark it down." I scowled at him and took a gulp of root beer.

"Your Shoppers left fielder . . . Milt Shoop!" boomed the announcer. The big left-handed batter strode to the plate. The big question: Could I do it again?

This time I penciled in a full diamond with a dot at the bottom. I put a 9 in the lower-left-hand

27

corner. And in the middle, I wrote the letters *HR*. Home run to right.

Then I erased the *9* and changed it to *8*. Shoop was a pretty good hitter. Why not see if he could poke it over the center-field fence?

Strike one, called. "Got to swing at it to hit it!" shouted the guy in the DUMB BOZO hat. I looked out toward the flag in center. It was dead still. The Dan's Supermarkets sign below it in straight-away center was where I wanted the ball to go out.

Faria shuffled down the line a little as the pitcher delivered. Ball one, way outside. Nice stop by the catcher to save a run. Faria hustled back to third.

Maybe not the Dan's sign, I thought, looking out toward center. I'll settle for the Caliente Mexican-American Restaurant sign a little bit toward right. That still counts as center field.

Shoop stepped out and stepped back in. The pitcher nodded at the catcher, wound, fired. Low. Ball two. The catcher jiggled his bare hand in a "get the ball up" gesture as he tossed the ball back.

I checked the flag again. It was billowing a little toward right.

Two and one. Shoop cranked the bat back and forth across the plate, then held it almost straight up. Big curve. Big swing. Foul tip. Strike two.

The umpire turned the ball over, made sure it was okay. The Shoppers mascot — a guy in a cash register suit — danced on the first-base dugout and started the fans clapping, "We want a hit! We want a hit!"

A loud crack! The visitors' dugout woke up and went scrambling as a screaming line foul nearly took somebody's head off. You could see the players loosen up, laugh, make faces, kid around.

Shoop looked serious now, dug his spikes into the dirt, swung the bat low over the plate. Tollefson looked in, took the sign, wound, threw.

Shoop reared back and swung from his heels. You could see the power in his arms as the bat whipped through the air. But it missed the ball entirely.

"Stee-rike three!" bellowed the umpire with a jab of his right hand.

"You're a bum, Shoop!" hollered a voice behind me.

I flipped over my pencil and began erasing the home run that didn't happen.

"Mistake?" my grandmother asked.

"I got confused," I muttered.

It was the absolute truth. As I put a *K* where the home run had been, I was confused, all right.

29

I was as confused as I had ever been in my entire life.

I didn't get around to trying out my magic again that inning. Before I even had a chance to think about it, Dexter Horton, the Shoppers designated hitter, sent a slow roller to the first baseman. Out number three. I marked it on the scorecard and stared at the Shoppers first inning. The way I figured, I just might have been personally responsible for the first half of it.

		R	H	E
Visitors	0	0	0	0
Shoppers	0	0	1	0

Top of the Second

"Shopper fans, turn to the Suttler's Jewelry page of your scorecard. If you have the green 'winner' stamp in the upper-left-hand corner, you've won a pair of beautiful twenty-four-karat gold earrings and a diamond bracelet."

Randy leaned across Grandma and snorted at me. "Bet you'd look great in those."

"Your grandmother would," Gramps said. "Did you win?"

I checked. "Guess."

"Better luck next time," Gramps said. "Got any nachos left?"

The nachos were getting to that stage where the cheese turns cold and stretches like melted rubber bands. I had been so distracted I'd forgotten to eat them up, which is pretty unusual for me. When I passed the tray along, my grandfather gave it a kind of dirty look, but when it comes to food, he's the one I got my genes from.

31

Gramps and I will eat just about anything. Even rubberized nachos.

As Dirk Wade finished his warmup tosses, I kept wondering what was going on. The whole thing was probably some sort of coincidence. This scorecard business couldn't really be happening. I mean, it was just two plays. Pure chance. Had to be. Had to be.

Ollie Raspberry was the Apples center fielder, a big guy with thighs the size of fire hydrants and a butt that stuck out like a shelf. He was the cleanup batter, and he definitely looked the part.

I checked the stat sheet. Power hitter, all right. Twenty-two home runs. Okay, fine. If I really could do what I wasn't sure I could do, maybe I could cool him off a little. So I put him down for a backward *K*, which stands for "struck out swinging." My grandmother says it's backward because it looks like a swinging door.

Wade reared back and threw. He nearly hit Raspberry, but I heard the tick of the bat and watched the ball roll foul. Strike one.

As the catcher tossed the ball back to Wade, my grandmother stuck the eraser end of her pencil on my scorecard and pointed at the swinging-door *K* I had penciled in. "Jake, what are you doing?"

I decided to play dumb. "What do you mean?"

Wade delivered ball one, low.

"It's one and one on the batter," Grandma said. "But you have him striking out already."

"I told you I was confused," I said.

"Go on, erase that. He's still up."

We watched a foul scream in our direction, but way over our heads.

"It's like last time," I said. "And now he's got two strikes on him. Maybe he really will strike out."

"Suit yourself." Grandma shrugged and shook her head. I guess she thought I was doing some sort of kid thing just to be stupid.

Ball two, way outside. The next pitch, I told myself. The next pitch. But the next pitch was high, ball three.

All right. Three and two. This was it. Now we'd see for sure. But Ollie Raspberry fought off the pitch with another line foul.

Still three and two. Wade shook off a sign. He wound. He threw. Raspberry started to swing, but held back. Ball four, called the umpire, and Raspberry jogged toward first base.

Right. My "magic" was as silly as I suspected it had to be. Or maybe — hey, who knew? — it only worked on *our* batters. "See that, smarty-pants?" Grandma said.

But just as she was saying it, Steel, our catcher,

appealed to the umpire behind first base. With a big wave of his thumb, the ump made the out sign. Yes, he was saying, Raspberry went around. It was a strikeout after all.

Raspberry couldn't believe it. He tossed his batting helmet on the ground and charged the first-base ump, bellowing all the way.

I couldn't believe it, either. The magic was there, after all. It really was. It worked on their batters as well as it worked on ours. It was too amazing to be true!

"Where did you ever learn to make a call like that?" I heard Raspberry scream at the first-base umpire. The Apples first-base coach grabbed his player and held him back, but he wouldn't stop shouting.

The umpire calmly threw up his hands, turned his back on those rotten Apples, and walked away. The coach walked Raspberry halfway back to the plate, and Raspberry had a few words with the umpire there, too. But that didn't change the fact that he was out.

Or that I had been right again. Once Raspberry sat down and the umpires got back into position, the PA system announced Apples third baseman Slade Gruber. "He's just a goober!" Randy yelled as Gruber menacingly loosened and tightened his grip on the bat. Wade looked in for his sign. Me, I began wondering what I could try next.

I mean, it still could have been just coincidence. It was no big deal for two guys to strike out, and people sometimes do hit triples even when they don't have much speed. I needed to figure out what was going on. I was trying to think what it would take to prove to me that I wasn't just making lucky guesses.

But before I could do that, Gruber slapped a little roller down the third-base line. Our third baseman, Tim Bakanauskas, ran it down, bare-handed it, and flipped it to first. It's a play minor leaguers hardly ever make, but this time was different. Faria made the big stretch to dig out the low throw, and Gruber was gone 5–3. "Nice play!" hollered my grandfather.

"Way to go, Timmy!" my grandmother added.

Up came the Apples catcher, Bret Klunder. Klunder was a chunky guy with kind of a cocky look and a giant wad of bubble gum that made his wide mouth look even wider. And as he blew a huge bubble, I figured out what it would take to convince me, the ultimate skeptic.

I would put down a one-in-a-million play, the kind you only see maybe once every ten years. I thought of a play I'd seen on TV. It was one of the biggest hits of the highlight films a few years ago, around the time that left fielder in the minors ran right through the outfield wall in a hail of splinters. It went pitcher to second to short to first.

I wrote it down: *1–4–6–3*. If this happened, I knew, this scorecard and I definitely had some kind of strange magical powers.

"No thunder for Klunder!" Randy yelled. The batter took called strike one, right down the middle. He fouled one off against the backstop. He took ball one, wide, and then ball two.

And then he cracked his bat on a shot up the middle off Dirk Wade's glove. Hernandez, our second baseman, came in and picked it up, but he was too far off line to make the play, so he flipped the ball to the shortstop charging across. Garis, the shortstop, fired it to Faria in plenty of time to nail the slow-running catcher.

1–4–6–3. Three up, three down. Big roar from the stands.

I felt like turning to the crowd and tipping my cap in thanks for all that applause.

		R	H	E
Visitors	00	0	0	0
Shoppers	0	0	1	0

Bottom of the Second

"Shoppers fans, please check your ticket stubs. We're about to award our next special Fan Appreciation Night prize: a mountain bike, courtesy of Vic's Velocipede Village. We're looking for the person sitting in section five" — hey, that was ours — "row three" — ours again! — "seat . . ." — Randy and I looked at each other in amazement — "nine."

We were in seats 1 through 4. At the other end of the row, a large woman in a cap with a tractor on it threw her hands in the air in a victory sign.

"Close," Randy said.

"Only counts in shaving," Grandma said.

"Luck's closing in on us," Randy insisted. "Any one of us could be the next winner."

"Or the next loser," I was going to say, but I didn't. Little did he know. Little did he know. Hey, I had a "guaranteed lucky" scorecard.

"Your Shoppers catcher: Zane Steel!" boomed the PA system.

"All right! Man of Steel!" my brother hollered. "Just a hit. Nothing zany!" Grandma and Gramps and I just shook our heads. Randy tended to say the same things every time certain batters came to the plate.

And I figured, what the hey! It's rally time here at Harold Errichetti Memorial Stadium! No sense being greedy. I had a whole game left to go.

I marked two sides of the diamond and put a 7 in the upper-right-hand corner. Any second now, Zane Steel would put all his might into a huge swing and blister a gapper to left for a double.

I felt like I was playing one of those computer games or board games where you get to be the manager. Only this time I wasn't just the manager: I was the God of Baseball. I could see the double in my mind. I leaned forward and waited for it to happen. Then I remembered to put my hand on the scorecard so Grandma wouldn't get annoyed again.

Ball one, in the dirt. "X-ray vision!" Randy shouted. A couple of people behind us laughed.

Steel dug in again. Ball two, way high.

I looked out toward left center. I figured the ball ought to roll up against the Sassini's Deli sign, or maybe the one for Eyes For You optometrists. I looked toward the mound. Tollefson delivered: ball three, behind Steel's back.

Klunder, the Apples catcher, went out to the mound. As far as I was concerned, it didn't matter. There couldn't be a ball four. I was sure of it. The way I had it figured, Steel would maybe take one down the middle, then drill the next pitch to left the way I had it marked beneath my hand. "Pitcher's crackin' up!" Randy sang.

I leaned behind Grandma to talk to him. "I guarantee you. He'll get this one over."

Randy leaned behind her to stare at me. "How much you want to bet?" he mouthed silently, moving his thumb and forefinger together to signify money.

"I hope you two aren't talking about me behind my back," Grandma said.

I suddenly realized this could get interesting. I reached into my pocket and held up two quarters.

Randy extended his hand behind Grandma. We shook on it. But as Klunder trotted back behind the plate, I realized I hadn't thought of all the possibilities. Maybe Tollefson wouldn't get the pitch over, but Steel would reach out and cream it anyway. Knowing Randy, we could be arguing about that one for weeks.

Tollefson toed the rubber and went into his windup. There were only two possibilities: a strike of some sort or the two-bagger I had hidden beneath my hand.

The pitch bounced a foot in front of the plate. "Ball four!" bellowed the umpire. Randy leaned behind Grandma and with a too-happy look made the money sign again.

"Later," I muttered as I erased the double that didn't happen and penciled in the walk that did. "I'm trying to keep score here."

"Take your time," Randy said. "I don't start charging interest till after the game."

I didn't say anything. I was trying to figure out what to do next. I knew *something* was going on: That 1–4–6–3 play had proved it. But how come I could make things happen sometimes, and other times I got a big zero? I was going to have to do some heavy thinking to figure all this out.

Mack Lenihan, the lanky, handsome center fielder for the Shoppers, came up to the plate with a determined look beneath his moustache. Across the field, the crowd chanted as the human cash register danced on the Apples dugout and held up a big sign that read LET's Go and a little sign that read MACK! I decided to just relax and watch the next play while I mulled things over.

The third-base coach relayed a flurry of signs. First his index finger across his chest, and then a tug on his cap, a hand on his left leg, and a pull on his right earlobe. "He's telling Lenihan to lay down a bunt," Gramps said. "And they know it. See how far in the first and third basemen are playing?"

"Hey, Steel!" Randy bellowed toward first base. "How about a steal!" Steel had to have heard, but he didn't take his eyes off the pitcher. One of the things that always amazed me about baseball players was the way they could shut out the crowd, even though with the stands so close to the field you knew they had to be hearing it.

Randy was only kidding. Steel was no baserunning threat, not with his chunky physique. The pitch came in. Lenihan squared to bunt but missed. Strike one.

I was still trying to figure out this scorecard business. I went through it in my head over and over again. It had worked in the bottom of the first (except when it hadn't). It had worked in the top of the second. Now it didn't seem to work at all. What was I doing wrong?

The next pitch was a little low, and Lenihan

missed another bunt attempt. The coach came in to talk with him, then ran back toward third.

"Do they take the bunt off with two strikes?" Randy wondered.

"I don't think so," I said. "I think they keep it on."

"How much you want to bet?"

"No bet," I said.

"That's right. You only bet on sure things. Sure losers."

"I've won a few," I reminded him.

"Very few."

The pitch came in, and Lenihan squared to bunt again. This time he made contact — the worst possible kind of contact. The ball popped into the air, and the catcher grabbed it. He nearly pegged Steel out diving back into first.

"Should've bet," Randy said.

"Maybe next time," I told him.

Up came Bakanauskas, the Shoppers third baseman. There was something about Bakanauskas I really liked. He was full of energy, always moving, always looking as though he was going to do something great. Unfortunately, his stats were crummy.

In a way, he kind of reminded me of me. I was always striking out and making errors, but I thought a lot of the time I looked pretty good doing them, though I admit Randy and some other people had lower opinions of my playing style, which I won't bother to repeat.

I decided what Bakanauskas needed was a double to right. I penciled it in. I decided to give him an RBI, so I moved Steel around from first to home on the scorecard. But by now I wasn't convinced it would actually happen.

Maybe that was it, I thought. Maybe I needed to be more confident. But I'd been totally confident about Steel and his double, and look what had happened: nothing.

And then I thought, Tollefson hadn't given Steel any pitches over the plate. Maybe that was the problem. Maybe when it came to our team, the batter needed to get at least one good pitch before my magic would work. Sure. That had to be it. All Bakanauskas would need was one good pitch. And my help.

Bakanauskas swung the bat back and forth in a slow, easy way. Tollefson looked the runner back, then burned one in with a sidearm delivery. Bakanauskas swung. He made good contact, and the ball bounced up the middle. But Pete Piccolini, the Apples shortstop, made a diving catch and flipped the ball to Ruidoso at second. He fired it on to Pelc the giant at first.

Well, it was sort of a double. It was a double play. Maybe I hadn't lost my touch after all.

		R	H	E
Visitors	**00**	0	0	0
Shoppers	**00**	0	1	0

Top of
the Third

"Shoppers fans," said the announcer, "please turn to the Eyes For You ad on page thirty-two of your scorecard."

"Don't bother," said Randy. "You already lost." Of course, that just made me turn to it quicker.

"If you have a red 'winner' stamp," said the announcer, "you've won one hundred dollars' worth of eye care."

"Now, no jokes about the umpires," Grandma said.

I looked at the page. I had won no hundred dollars' worth of anything. "Amazing prediction, Rand. You should join those telephone psychics who advertise on TV. You could give people advice like, 'You won't win a prize tomorrow.' "

"Or even the day after that," Randy said. "Third-inning shift!" He climbed over Grandma, and she moved down so my brother could sit

45

beside me. We did this at just about every game. It was sort of a family tradition.

The PA system at the park went flaky now and then. This time it was so filled with static, you could hardly hear the name of the batter. But of course, I'd filled out the lineup before the game, so I knew the batter was number 26, Dave Karasik, the Apples right fielder.

What I didn't know for sure was whether I could make him fly out to right, which is what I had marked on the scorecard while Grandma and Randy were changing seats. If confidence was the key, it wasn't going to happen. I didn't have any confidence about it at all.

"Hey, what's going on?" Randy mumbled in my ear.

I covered the scorecard with my hand as Karasik took a big swing for big strike one. "What do you mean, 'What's going on?' "

"Not so loud," Randy mumbled back. "Grandma and Gramps might hear."

"Hear what?" I said under my breath.

"I've been watching you. You've been up to something."

"Like what?"

"Something. Something. I can't figure it out totally yet, but you're up to some darned thing."

I didn't even look toward my brother. Ball one on Karasik.

"Hey, let me see the scorecard a second," Randy said.

"I thought you didn't believe in keeping score."

"Just for a second. I didn't catch the name of the batter."

"David Karasik," I said without looking down or moving my hand. "Right field."

Somebody tapped me on the left shoulder, and I turned to look. That's when I felt the scorecard being yanked right out of my hands. Randy was a master at the old reach-behind-you-and-tap-you-on-the-far-shoulder-to-make-you-look trick. And I had fallen for it one more time.

"Give me that," I muttered.

"One second," he said, holding the scorecard away from me and staring at it.

"Come on!"

And then I heard the crack of the bat. At first I had no idea where the ball had gone, but as Gramps had told me thousands of times, when you're a fan, don't watch the ball, watch the fielders. So I watched the fielders, and the way they were running told me to look down the line in right field. And the instant after I found Duke

Mountain, he reached up and pulled down a high fly ball. The God of Baseball — me! — was back in business. At least, if my brother's cooties hadn't given my scorecard some kind of terrible disease.

"Give me the scorecard," I demanded.

He held it away from me and nearly hit Grandma.

"Come on, Randy. Give it to him," she said.

He handed it back. Then he leaned toward me, pointed to Karasik's box on the scorecard, and whispered in my ear. "What's that?"

I played dumb. "What's what?"

"That nine there. I think it's kind of interesting that the play happened while I was holding the scorecard, but somehow you already had it written down."

I played dumber. "That is strange, all right."

"Crazy luck," Randy said.

"It's not luck," I told him.

"Sure it's not! Like you can control the game or something!"

Yeldon Fenneman, the Apples designated hitter, was stepping into the batter's box. Fenneman had a huge head and no neck at all. "He's gonna hit a liner to the third baseman," I told Randy. "Or a popup. Third base unassisted one way or the other."

48

"Oh, sure," Randy said.

"How much you want to bet?" I demanded.

"Same fifty cents."

Fenneman took a ball inside. "Deal," I said. Then I scribbled the number 5 in Fenneman's frame for the third inning. I didn't even bother to hide it from Randy. I sort of wanted him to see what I was doing.

"Pretty confident, aren't you?" he said.

"I can always erase."

Fenneman foul-tipped one off Steel's mask. "Ouch! That must hurt!" Gramps declared.

Steel took off his mask, worked his jaw from side to side, and walked around.

"Maybe next pitch?" Randy sneered.

"I didn't say I could tell which pitch. I said third base, unassisted."

Steel shook his head, put the mask back on, and got into his crouch. "Man of Steel!" somebody bellowed from the crowd. The pitcher fired. Ball two, just outside.

I needled Randy. "You still think the third baseman won't make the play?"

"Right you are, youngster." Randy knew I hated it when he called me "youngster."

"Want to double the bet?" I asked.

"Sure." Randy thought about it. "This pitch?"

"I told you, I don't know which one it'll — "

Crack! A hot line drive straight to third. Bakanauskas didn't have to move a step.

I gave Randy a big smile. "You're down a dollar."

"Half a dollar," Randy said. "You owe me from that other bet."

Pete Piccolini, the Apples' skinny shortstop, stepped up to the plate. "Double or nothing," I said. "I'll call this one, too."

"Something fishy's going on, Jake."

"Double or nothing. Put up or shut up."

"Okay. Double or nothing it is."

"Catcher to first." As the pitcher looked in for his signs, I marked down *2–3* in Pete Piccolini's box for the third inning. As Wade got set to throw, I pointed the box out to my brother.

"What's the deal?" Randy demanded.

"For me to know and you to find out, youngster."

Piccolini hit a little dribbler that died in front of home plate. I knew I was about to make two dollars. Steel tore off his mask, grabbed the ball, and threw down to first. Three up, three down.

"Don't look now, but Wade has a no-hitter going." Randy didn't say a word about our bet.

"Through three! Big deal!" I said.

"It's supposed to be bad luck to mention it," my grandmother pointed out.

"Oh, that's another one of those stupid baseball superstitions," said my grandfather. "Besides, it's not just a no-hitter. Wade's working
on a perfect game."

What Gramps didn't know was that I was
working on it, too.

		R	H	E
Visitors	000	0	0	0
Shoppers	00	0	1	0

Bottom of the Third

"Shoppers fans, it's time for The Great Race, sponsored by your friends at the First Bank of Nottingham and starring our amazing grounds-keeper, Eddie Sundstrom!"

Sundstrom was a short, squat guy in an out-rageous neon-orange tracksuit with the bank's big "1" logo on it. He wore sunglasses that were about three times as wide as his face. He held his hands over his head in a victory gesture at first base. The crowd cheered.

"On second base tonight, selected from our audience, Mr. Wayne Gwaltney of Mount Lopez!" Gwaltney was a tall, gangly kid a couple of years older than Randy. The crowd gave him a big cheer, too.

"As always, our challenger will begin on sec-ond base and may run, walk, slide, or even crawl. As always, our Great Racer must keep one foot on the ground at all times in a walking gait. Our challenger's goal is to try to beat our Great Racer around the base paths to home plate and win a two-hundred-and-fifty-dollar savings account from the First Bank of Nottingham. Are you ready, Great Racer?"

They did this every night, and it sounded dorky when you told people about it. Actually it was a lot of fun, because Sundstrom was very good at it. He gave the thumbs-up sign from first.

"Are you ready, challenger?" The challenger waved his fist in the air.

"If you're such a hotshot, maybe you can predict who'll win this," Randy scoffed.

"Sorry. Only the game," I said.

"Come on. Who's gonna win?"

"Not you!"

My brother gave me a poke.

"On your marks! Get set! Go!" The PA system began playing chase music. The challenger got a good start from second, but Sundstrom's long strides gobbled up the distance from first.

"Think he'll catch up?" my brother wondered.

"He almost always does," I said.

"Anybody want to bet on it?" Randy inquired.

"Randy, are your parents raising you to be a riverboat gambler?" Gramps asked.

The challenger was nearing third. The Great Racer was flapping his elbows, pumping his legs like some kind of robot. And closing in.

The challenger made the third-base turn a little too wide, but the Great Racer pivoted around third perfectly. Now he poured it on, the crowd roared, and Wayne Gwaltney dove for the plate in a big headfirst slide — an instant after Sundstrom had already crossed it.

"Nice try, Wayne," said the announcer. "And for being such a good sport, you'll get a free meal at any of four Taco Casa locations! So the Great Racer closes out this Shoppers baseball and race-walking season with forty-one victories and five defeats! Let's give them both a big Shoppers hand!"

As the crowd applauded and the umpire dusted off the plate with his little whisk broom, Randy leaned over to me and muttered, "You mind if I try one?"

"One what?" I said softly so that Grandma and Gramps wouldn't hear.

"One play. Like I'll pick it and you'll write it down. Not that I really believe it'll work."

I shook my head as Lamont Garis was announced for the Shoppers. Garis was a pretty good hitter for a shortstop, but he made a lot of throwing errors. A lot of guys in the minors made a lot of throwing errors.

"Why not?" Randy said.

"It won't work," I told him.

"How do you know it won't work?"

"I've tried. I can't get it to work on our guys anymore."

"What do you mean?"

"Like if I put down a hit for Garis, he probably won't get one."

"Try it. Make it a single to right."

I shrugged. "It only works when we're in the field. It used to work for our batters, but it doesn't anymore."

"If it worked once, it'll work again."

"No. I think I've only got half an inning's worth of magic every inning. Maybe just three batters' worth. It's all used up for this inning."

"Try it. Single to right."

Sometimes there's just no arguing with Randy. I put down a single to right. A second later, Lamont Garis turned on the first pitch and cracked a line drive to left, just over the head of the third baseman. It was good for a double.

"Well, he got a hit," my brother said.

"A double to left is not the same thing as a single to right," I pointed out. I erased the single from the scorecard and changed it to a double.

"Your Shoppers second baseman . . . Hector Hernandez!" boomed the PA system.

"Give 'em heck, Hector!" shouted a little guy behind us. Hernandez was a crowd favorite. According to the local paper, he was the shortest player in organized baseball. He didn't get a lot of hits, but with his tiny strike zone he did walk a lot, and he was pretty slick in the field.

"Okay," said my brother. "Give Hector a single to — oh, let's say center."

"And that way maybe he'll get a triple?"

"Exactly my idea."

I made a face, but I did it. Hector Hernandez, single to center. Sure.

Hector took two strikes and a ball. Then he began fouling pitches off. He fouled one high over the press box. He fouled one down the third-base line. He fouled one off his foot and danced around awhile. He drew ball two.

He fouled a pitch off the edge of the visitors' dugout. He fouled one over our heads, about ten rows back. He sent a towering pop foul just out of reach of the Apples right fielder in the stands behind the bullpen. He drew ball three. And then he drew ball four.

"Great at bat!" hollered my grandfather. "Way to go!"

"Runners on first and second, nobody out," Randy muttered to me. "Now how about a home run?"

"A home run?" I was erasing furiously. "Hey, your double didn't even work."

"We got a man on, right?"

"We got a walk, not a single."

"Almost as good, man, almost as good. And here's Duke Mountain. If he can't do it, nobody can."

"Nobody can," I said, just to get his goat. I think I mentioned that Duke Mountain was Randy's favorite Shopper.

"How many home runs has he had so far this year?" Randy challenged me.

"Eight or ten. I forget."

"Twelve," Randy said firmly.

I checked the stat sheet. "Okay. Twelve."

"I know my man. And now's the time. Three-run blast. Dead center."

I looked at Randy. "Come on," he said. "Write it down."

"This is the last one," I said. "No home run, you're out of luck."

"Guaranteed home run."

"The guarantee with the Shoppers is if I write it down, it doesn't happen."

Mountain took ball one, just outside.

"Home run. I guarantee it." Randy said firmly.

"With what?"

"A giant popcorn."

"Huh?"

"You write it down. If it doesn't happen, you get a giant popcorn."

I wrote it down. Why not? If it worked, great. If not, and I was sure it wouldn't, I'd win the popcorn.

Duke Mountain took big roundhouse swings at the next two pitches. He wasn't even close. "Nice cut, Man Mountain!" Randy yelled the first time. "Getting closer, Mountain Man!" he hollered the second time.

"What are you going to yell the next time?" I asked.

Randy smiled and stared at me. "I'm going to yell, 'It's outta here!'"

Mountain took a ball low and away. "Good eye, Volcano Man!" Randy hollered. "Now it's tater time!"

The next pitch was a fast ball right down the middle of the plate. It was a perfect home-run ball. But Mountain only got some of it and chopped a grounder toward third. Gruber, the Apples third baseman, stayed with it, stepped on the bag, and nailed Mountain at first. Double play. At least it sent Hernandez down to second.

"Some home run," I muttered. As I flipped my pencil over, I wondered if the eraser would hold up.

Randy looked kind of deflated. "Nice try, Duke!" he yelled kind of halfheartedly. Mountain stormed into the dugout with a swearword on his lips.

As Tollefson went back to the mound, Hernandez danced his way into a big lead off second, and Tony Faria stepped into the batter's box. I noticed the shortstop sneaking over toward second. Weingartner, our coach, noticed it, too, and he hollered from first as Tollefson whirled and threw.

Hernandez dived for second, but the ball got there first. Piccolini tagged him out.

"Nice pickoff, darn it!" said my grandfather.

No runs, one hit, no errors, no men left on base. And no help from this crazy scorecard of mine.

		R	H	E
Visitors	000	0	0	0
Shoppers	000	0	2	0

Top of the Fourth

"Let's go get that popcorn," my brother sighed.

"You kidding?" I said. "In the middle of a perfect game? No way am I going to miss this."

"All right. End of next inning then. Three inning perfect game. Big deal."

"You know I don't leave my seat when I'm scoring a game. *You* bring back the popcorn."

"End of next inning. Maybe. I want to see the perfect game, too."

"Shoppers fans, it's hot dog time, time for those great wieners from Fantell's Franks. Please turn to the inside back cover of your souvenir program. If there's a picture in red of a smiling hot dog, you've won yourself fifty pounds of Fantell's Franks, the official wiener of the Nottingham Shoppers."

"You're the unofficial wiener of the Nottingham Shoppers," Randy said, grabbing me in a neck hold and giving me a head rub.

"*You* are," I told him as I broke free. "And just for that, I'm not going to split my wienings with you."

"Half of nothing is nothing," Randy said.

"You just wait," I said as I opened the cover. No prize, of course, but Randy took out a pen and aimed it at the Fantell's Franks ad. I knew he was going to draw a smiling hot dog — it had been a running joke between us just about every game — but this time I thought it might spoil whatever luck it was that this program had. I moved the program away from him.

"Hey, no happy wiener?"

"Not now. Not while I'm figuring out what's going on here."

Wade looked pretty good as he took his warm-up pitches, though a couple of them landed in the dirt. Reynaldo Ruidoso tossed his batting donut into the on-deck circle and strode up to the plate for his second at bat. Maybe I was imagining it, but I thought I could see him thinking that it was time to get serious. It was time, he told himself, to break up Wade's little perfecto.

And it was up to me to see that didn't happen. I penciled in a 7 for a fly out to left. Ruidoso swung at the first pitch and sent a high pop just where I had planned it. Shoop reeled it in. One away.

"Nice going," said Randy. "Can I try one?"

"Why not?" I knew enough about Randy to know that if I didn't let him pick at least one play, he'd hound me until I did. I just hoped it wouldn't kill the magic and Wade's perfect game.

"Okay: six to three. Routine grounder to short."

I wrote it down as Covington came up to the plate. Wade brushed him back with a fast ball inside. Ball one. "How come you don't have any control over *when* they hit it?" Randy asked.

"How come anything?" I told him. "How should I know? Maybe it's because I don't keep balls and strikes." I don't do it, and Grandma doesn't, either. I've tried. If you miss a single pitch, and you always do, your scorecard is out of whack. It's just too hard to be that good unless you're the official scorekeeper or a scout or some kind of pro.

"Maybe you should start. That way you can have guys make outs sooner. Wade won't get so tired."

"I didn't start keeping balls and strikes, and I'm not about to start now." Covington took a big swing at a low curve that would've been ball two. "It's too much work. Besides, it might change things."

"Suit yourself, lazybones," said Randy. "Just trying to help."

"In case you didn't notice, I'm doing pretty well without your help."

Covington hit a pop foul so high that half the people in our part of the stands covered their heads or ducked. It landed with a thunk on the grandstand roof, then bounced out.

"I just hope I didn't screw things up by letting you have a turn," I said.

"Six–three," Randy said. "I guarantee it."

"You still owe me that popcorn and the dollar and a half."

"Six–three," he repeated.

And then Ben Covington bounced a soft two-hopper to Garis at short. Nothing to it. 6–3. Out number two.

"It's too bad you can't do stuff for the Shoppers, too," Randy said thoughtfully. "That would really be fun."

"What's not fun about this?"

"You don't want to break up this perfect game."

"So?"

"So we can't even put down a hit. Not even a walk. Not even some weird play like a goofy error."

"True."

Randy grabbed my pencil. "Let me write one in?"

Fred Pelc came up to the plate. "Are you kidding? I have no idea what might happen."

"Won't know till I try."

"It might take everything away. Forget it! Forget it! And give me back my pencil!"

"Okay, okay. Wade's in his windup. Foul out to right. Quick!"

I wrote down *9F* just as the ball hit the dirt in front of the plate. Ball one.

"You just want to see Mountain come running over here."

Randy grinned. "You bet I do."

Pelc fouled off a high pop way back into the seats behind us. "Homing in," Randy said.

Wade threw another high pitch that not even the catcher could stop. The crowd kind of gasped. They were getting into it. Everybody was beginning to realize that Wade had his no-hitter and perfect game, even though it was not even four innings old.

Pelc fouled a long line drive into the left-field bleachers. The Shopper mascot was setting up shop on top of our dugout, and he smelled blood. The human cash register jumped up and down and started flashing cards for the crowd.

"STRIKE. OUT. STRIKE. OUT." The crowd got into it. "STRIKE! OUT! STRIKE! OUT!" Pelc fouled one off into the backstop.

"Hey, change it," Randy said.

"What do you mean change it?"

"The crowd wants a strikeout. Give him a strikeout."

"I don't want to."

"Hey, it's my at bat. I changed my mind. I want him to strike out."

"There isn't time," I protested as Wade went into his windup. "I'd have to erase it all and then put the strikeout in."

Wade fired the ball over the umpire's head for ball two. "Now there's time," Randy said.

"I don't know what will happen."

"Come on. Do it."

I did it. I erased the *9F* and penciled in a backward *K*.

And as Wade looked in for his sign, I suddenly remembered the last time I changed somebody's at bat. Back in the first inning I had Shoop homering to right. Then I changed it to center. What actually happened was that he struck out. I suddenly realized that erasing might not be a good idea.

Wade wound up. Pelc took the big swing that was supposed to be a backward *K*.

The ball had other ideas. It took off like a rocket toward the deepest part of center field. "Uh-oh," said my brother, and you could hear the crowd saying the same thing.

Mack Lenihan ran deep, deeper, deepest. At the warning track he turned and looked, jumped up against the wall, and thrust his glove in the air as high as he could. Then he came down, landed on his side, and waved the glove — with the ball in it.

I looked back. Pelc stopped halfway to second and raised his hands in the air as if he had just been robbed — which he had. The crowd went crazy. Out by the wall, Shoop helped Lenihan pick himself up. As he loped toward the dugout, he took the ball from his glove and waved it proudly. Finally he tossed it to the umpire.

"Look at Wade!" my grandfather shouted. Wade was running out toward Lenihan, grabbing his shoulders. From where we sat, Wade looked almost old enough to be Lenihan's dad.

"Pilgrim," said Randy, doing his John Wayne imitation, "you're on your own from here on out." And he patted me on the back.

He was right. If I could help it, I was never going to erase anything on that scorecard ever again. If I was going to help Wade preserve his perfect game, I realized, I'd have to have pretty close to a perfect game myself.

		R	H	E
Visitors	000 0	0	0	0
Shoppers	000	0	2	0

Bottom of the Fourth

"Shoppers fans, it's time for the Elephant Peanuts Peanut Toss. We hope you all know the rules." We knew them, all right. Somebody got picked from the crowd to throw sacks of peanuts through the mouth of a clown painted on a little board. "Tonight's lucky contestant is Gina Tarkusian from the town of Mallicoom. She'll take home five dollars for every delicious bag of Elephant Peanuts she can feed the clown in sixty seconds. Are you ready, Gina?"

"Ready!" she screamed.

"Then go!"

Circus music played as she tossed the peanuts toward the hole. "Lame!" said Randy when fifteen seconds had gone by and she hadn't gotten credit for a single bag. A couple of nights before, some guy had thrown thirty bags in for the record, but that wasn't Fan Appreciation Night, so he only got two dollars a bag. Gina was so bad

I almost wished there was some way my score-card and I could help her out.

"Shutout?" Gramps wondered with thirty seconds to go. But Gina started to find her form. "One!" shouted the crowd. "Two! Three! Four! Five! Whoa!" She missed one. "Six! Seven! Eight! Oh!" She missed another one. The music played faster. "Nine! Ten! Eleven! Twelve! Thirteen!"

The music stopped. "A lucky thirteen! Sixty-five dollars for the young lady from Mallicoom! Let's give her a big Shoppers hand!"

Tollefson finished his warmup tosses. Since Hernandez had been thrown out during Faria's at bat, Faria was back to lead off the inning. I was still feeling cheated about the erasing business. If I'd left well enough alone, Pelc would have fouled out to right just the way Randy and I originally planned it.

I thought about it a little more. Because I had done that erasing, I had only influenced what had happened to two batters in the top of the fourth. If I really got to control three batters per inning — I still wasn't sure about this, but so far it seemed that way — then maybe the scorecard still owed me one.

Anyway, it seemed to be worth a try. We needed some runs and nobody was doing the job. I put Faria down for a homer to left.

"I thought it didn't work for our side," Randy blurted out.

"Quiet," I muttered. "I don't want Grandma or Gramps to hear about this."

"Well, I thought it didn't."

"Just be quiet, okay? I have an idea I'm trying out. Where's the money you owe me? And that popcorn?"

Faria took a huge swing at a ball that looked great but dropped out of the strike zone at the last minute. Strike one.

"I'm not the popcorn delivery service," Randy said.

"I told you, I need to keep score."

"All right, all right." He turned to Grandma and Gramps. "I'm going for popcorn. You guys want anything?"

Faria took a pitch outside. Ball one.

"Get a big one so we all can share," Gramps said.

Great, I thought. If we all share, maybe Grandma and Gramps will notice what is going on.

"One?" Randy said. "That may not be enough with Fats here" — meaning me. Faria took ball two.

"Then you can get a fresh one later," Gramps said, and handed Randy some money. I wanted to complain, because this was supposed to be a private popcorn deal between Randy and me, but I knew it wouldn't be any use. My grandparents are retired, and when my parents say they shouldn't be spending so much money on us, Grandma and Gramps always say they hardly have anything else to spend it on. When my mom and dad come to pick us up, they always say my grandparents have spoiled us, whatever that's supposed to mean.

Faria took ball three. "See you next inning," Randy said as he stepped over me.

"Just bring back that popcorn," I told him. I was beginning to work up an appetite.

Gramps climbed over Grandma and sat down where Randy had been. "Faria should get one to hit now."

I covered Faria's home run in my scorecard. "If this pitcher can ever get the ball over the plate."

"You've got a point," Gramps said. "Well, a walk's as good as a hit."

Tollefson bounced one into the dirt. Ball four.

Darn. I should've known I wasn't going to get that extra credit. And now I had to erase the home run I had given Faria. I tried to do it when Gramps wasn't looking.

But Gramps had an awfully good eye. "What's

that there?" he asked me as the pink rubber elim-
inated the last traces of Faria's never-happened
homer.

As Shoop dug in at the plate, I put the walk
down and decided to play dumb again. "What's
what?"

"Didn't you have a home run in there for Faria?"

I shrugged. "Got confused."

"Your grandmother says you're getting confused quite a bit this game."

"I guess so," I said.

"I notice you're not putting anything down for
Shoop."

"Of course not. He hasn't hit yet." He missed
a bunt attempt for strike one.

"Well, neither had Faria."

"I told you. I was confused."

"Hmmm," said Gramps. "Think Shoop can lay
one down?"

I shrugged. "Why not?"

"Lenihan didn't. But then maybe this guy's
better."

"Hope so."

"Well, he ought to aim for third. That third
baseman's playing back too far."

I glanced toward third. When it came to watching baseball, Gramps didn't miss much.

Shoop squared around to bunt, and he laid it

down perfectly. The catcher barely nailed him at first, where the second baseman was covering. Faria motored into second. 2–4. One away.

"So now what?" Gramps sort of asked the air, almost as though he were talking to himself. I kept my mouth shut. "Come on. Any ideas?"

"Get a hit," I said. "Keep the ball on the right side of the infield."

"You don't seem confused. You're in the game."

Dexter Horton stood in. "Dex-TER! Dex-TER!" hollered the crowd, in time with the signs the Shoppers mascot held up.

"That guy is the hardest-working mascot in the business," Gramps said.

"Maybe because he's got the stupidest outfit," I said as Horton took ball one high.

"You've got a point there, Jake. Now let's see if we can get us some runs. What'd this guy do last time up?"

I kind of hid the scorecard from Gramps. "Made the last out of the first inning. Grounded out to the first baseman unassisted."

"Can I take a look?" he said as Horton took another pitch, a strike this time. I could hardly say no to him, but I tried to keep my hand over all the erasures. Gramps moved my hand so he could see better.

73

"You really did get confused," Gramps observed. "Especially that last inning." He looked back toward the game. "That's not like you. Usually your scorecards are nearly as clean as your grandmother's, except for the mustard. Whoa! Heads up!"

A foul ball screamed our way, but sliced about two boxes over. Nobody caught it on the fly, so it bounced off a railing and under some seats. After a mad scramble for the ball, a redheaded kid came up with it, and another kid grabbed it right out of his hand. The crowd started booing. A beer vendor made the second kid give the ball back to the first one.

"Fair play," Gramps said. "The other guy caught it fair and square. Fair play."

I wasn't sure, but I had the feeling he meant those words for me, as if I was being a poor sport or cheating somehow. On the mound, Tollefson delivered, and Horton blasted a high foul deep to left.

"Wrong way, wrong way!" my grandfather muttered as Covington loped toward the bleachers with his arm outstretched. As he neared the fence, a fan dumped a huge cup of beer all over him. The Apples left fielder got drenched, and the ball popped in and out of his glove.

The umpire called the batter out. My grandfather shook his head. "Fan interference."

"You mean they can call somebody out even if the fielder drops the ball?"

"Sure. It's in the rule book. The official term is spectator interference. You can't let fans get away with stuff like that." And he gave me a funny look.

Up came Steel. "Didn't you and Randy have a bet on that guy last time?"

"Yeah. I lost."

"How much?"

"Fifty cents." Ball one to Steel.

"I don't know if I approve of that. You could lose too much money."

"I won even more from him," I said, and suddenly wished I could suck the words back into my mouth. Strike one, foul.

"Interesting," Gramps said, taking a sip of his Coke. "How'd you do that?"

"Uh, we bet on another play." Strike two, foul.

"Just one?"

"Well, two, actually."

"And how'd you know what was going to happen?"

"It wasn't so much that I knew what was going to happen," I said. "It was that Randy didn't."

"Oh," Gramps said.

Called strike three on Steel. Out number three. End of inning. "You're a bum, Steel!"

I wanted to spill the beans. I wanted to tell him what I knew. I wanted to ask him if he knew why it was happening, and if it was happening, was it *right* for me to be doing what I was doing?

But I could guess what he'd say without even asking. "You can't always know what's right in life," he would say. "Life is complicated. It isn't a game where you're handed all the rules or where you're the good guy and the other guy's the bad guy. On the other hand, baseball is a game. It does have rules."

"But our team is the good guys. The other team is the bad guys," I would say.

And Gramps would shake his head. "Depends where you sit. There are seven other towns around here where the home team's the good guys, and the Shoppers are the bad guys. Do the Shoppers deserve to get help from a secret weapon?"

I could hear Grandma putting her two cents in. "Let's say the Shoppers could put cork in their bats to get fifteen extra feet on every line drive. And let's say they have a secret way to do it so they know they can get away with it. Should they do it?"

"That's cheating. It's against the rules."

"What if they could put something secret on the ball — something that would make it curve extra wide or take crazy dips, something totally invisible that no umpire could ever catch. What about that?"

"That's against the rules, too. Like a spitball."

"Okay. How about fan interference?" Gramps would say. "You *are* interfering, aren't you?"

And if you thought about it that way, I guess I *was* interfering. But the way I saw it, fooling around with this scorecard was different from dumping a beer on somebody. Besides, I didn't *want* to stop.

So I didn't ask, and Gramps didn't say a word.

		R	H	E
Visitors	000 0	0	0	0
Shoppers	000 0	0	2	0

Top of
the Fifth

"Shoppers fans, please turn to the Sassini's Deli ad on page twenty-five of your scorecard. If it shows the word 'Supersubmarine' stamped in purple, you've won six six-foot Supersubs, courtesy of Sassini's."

I checked. No Supersubmarine in purple, blue, or even Shoppers green and silver. "Better luck next inning," said my grandfather. "Right?"

Maybe I was just imagining it, but I thought there was something slightly suspicious about the way he said that. I was beginning to think he had figured out what I was doing, and I was pretty sure he wouldn't approve. "I'd better go pee," I announced. If I went somewhere, at least I'd be off the hook for awhile.

"I don't think you've ever left the seats before the seventh-inning stretch," Grandma said. "How are you going to keep score?"

"I'll check your scorebook when I get back," I said.

"Don't you want to wait till this half of the inning's over?" Grandma said. "Wade is still throwing" — she lowered her voice — "a perfect game."

"None of that superstition stuff," Gramps scolded.

I shrugged. "When you gotta go, you gotta go."

I headed for the tunnel to the stairway that led under the grandstand. But instead of going down to where the concession stands and rest rooms were, I stood in the tunnel, just far enough back so that my grandparents couldn't see me. I felt like a sneak.

But I didn't have time to worry about it. Raspberry, the Apples' big center fielder, was the first one up in the inning. It was a little tricky writing without anything to lean on, so I wrote down the easiest thing I could think of — *1*. Nothing fancy, just a single stroke. Pop out to the pitcher.

Raspberry fouled off one pitch. He took a ball low and away. He tipped one off the catcher's mitt. And then he absolutely creamed a line drive up the middle. Dirk Wade stuck his bare hand up in self-defense — and caught the ball! 1. Just 1, the way I had called it.

But not quite what I'd had in mind. That ball must really have stung. The second Wade put it into his glove, he started staring at his pitching hand and shaking it. Harley Hake, the Shoppers manager, rushed out from the bench to see if Wade was all right. The trainer went out, too, and there was a buzz in the crowd as he kept moving Wade's fingers back and forth, feeling them with his own fingers, looking at them closely. And I kept thinking, did I do that? Did I make this happen? Was this my fault? Please let him not be hurt.

"Hey, is he okay?" It was Randy, loaded down with popcorn and sodas.

"I hope."

"I heard it on some guy's radio. A real shot, huh?"

"Yeah. I meant it to be a popup."

Wade kept shaking his head as if to say, there's nothing wrong, let me pitch. The umpires joined the conference. After a minute or two, everybody backed away from Wade and watched as he threw a few warmups.

"What are you doing up here, anyway?" Randy asked.

"Kind of hiding out for a while."

"Hiding out?"

"I think they're getting suspicious," I told Randy through a mouthful of popcorn.

"Who?"

"Grandma and Gramps."

"I have a theory," Randy said.

"About what?"

"About why you can't get your scorecard to work for more than half an inning."

"Yeah?"

"Yeah. What if somebody else here has a score-card like yours?"

"Huh?"

"Let's say there's an Apples fan here. Let's say he's got a magic scorecard, too. Then maybe you're in competition. Maybe only one of you can have the magic at one time."

"Maybe there are UFOs," I said. "Some theory."

"It's just an idea. You have a better one?"

I shrugged.

"Besides, if you can do what you're doing, maybe there really *are* UFOs!"

Wade nodded to everybody that he was okay. The manager patted the pitcher on the butt and left the field. The crowd gave Wade a huge hand. The umpire scooted back to the plate, dusted it off, and hollered, "Play ball!" Slade Gruber stepped up to the plate.

"Take it easy," Randy said. "Don't put down any more shots to the pitcher, or that perfect game might be toast."

81

"I told you. I meant it to be a popup," I said as I put Gruber down for a ground out to second: 4–3. He took ball one.

"Just keep the ball away from Wade. What'd you do for this guy?"

Gruber took ball two. I showed Randy my scorecard.

"Better," he said. "And stay away from strike-outs for awhile till his hand stops stinging. No point in making him work any harder than he has to."

Ball three on Gruber. Maybe Wade had lost it after all. Randy took off with the popcorn and the drinks.

"Where you going?"

"Back to the seats!"

"Hey, leave me some!"

"No way! More for me!"

"Hey!"

But it was too late. Randy was gone.

Wade fired a fast ball right down the middle. Gruber took it for strike one. The crowd sent up a big cheer.

Next came a slow curve. Gruber got way out in front of it and dribbled it to second. Hernandez scooped it up and flipped to Faria. Two outs. Gruber ran back to the dugout shaking his head all the way.

Klunder, the Apples catcher, came up to the plate. I put down *2F* for him. Foul out to our catcher. From one catcher to the other. I kind of liked that.

And Klunder was first-pitch swinging. He got under the ball and lifted a high pop just behind the plate. Steel tossed his mask aside and looked up. No problem. Into the mitt for out number three.

But that giant root beer had done its work. Now I really did have to go to the bathroom. By the time I got back to the seats, that popcorn would probably be history.

			R	H	E
Visitors	000	00	0	0	0
Shoppers	000	0	0	2	0

Bottom of the Fifth

"Shoppers fans, please check your tickets. One lucky fan is about to win one hundred dollars worth of sporting equipment, courtesy of North Woods Sports. If you're sitting in section two . . ."

Well, so much for that. I headed through the exit and down the stairs. I made a left to head toward the bathroom. And I couldn't even get near it. There must've been forty people standing in a long line outside the door.

I stepped up behind a potbellied guy wearing a T-shirt that read FAT AND HAPPY and a cap with a cartoon of a moose on it. "Never saw anything like this line," he grumbled. "You could miss half the game."

"Must be the big crowd," I said, wondering what was happening on the field. "Usually I can get down here and back to my seat between innings."

"Usually!" He belched and shook his head.

The PA system was worse on this side of the stands. It just barely scratched out the announcement for Lenihan. The line inched forward, and a tall skinny guy with a scruffy gray beard got in line behind me. He was wearing one of those radios that clip to your ear so that the long antenna sticking out makes you look like half a Martian.

A huge roar went up from the stands. I figured it couldn't have been for the two people who came out of the rest room. "Foul ball," the guy behind me reported. "Right fielder just missed it."

"Way to go!" I said.

"Need some runs, that's what we need," muttered Potbelly, the guy in front of me.

"Ball one on Lenihan," said Graybeard, the man behind me, a second or two later. "Low and away."

"That guy is due," Potbelly said.

A sort of halfhearted cheer went up from the crowd. It was the kind of cheer you hear when somebody hits the ball but about all you can hope is the other team makes an error.

"Ground out to second," Graybeard announced. Potbelly shook his head. And I wrote 4–3 in Lenihan's box for the fifth inning.

Bakanauskas was up next. He was the kind of

guy who you wanted to be a hero once in awhile, just because he wasn't the kind of guy you expected to be one. I was hoping he'd get a hit, but I knew there wasn't anything I could do about it.

The low "oooh" from the stands meant the crowd didn't like the call. Must've been a close pitch. "Strike one, according to the umpire," Graybeard said sarcastically.

The line was just creeping. At this rate, there wasn't a chance I could get back in time for the next inning.

"Swung on and missed. Strike two," said Graybeard. I looked back. Now there were half a dozen people in line behind him. At least the line was moving, sort of.

I heard the distant crack of the bat and a muffled howl from the crowd. I looked toward the grandstand, and next thing I knew, I saw a baseball come down from half a mile in the air. It made a loud click and bounced high off the concrete. Then it came down again, right at me. I grabbed the ball with my bare hands. It stung a little. But it was mine!

A couple of people around me swore because they'd missed the ball, but some other people said, "Nice catch!" I'll say it was a nice catch!

I couldn't believe it. I had never been close to catching a ball all the times I had sat in the stands. Now I stood in the pee line, and the ball came right to me. Weird night, all right.

"You dropped this," said Potbelly as I stepped back into line. He handed me my program. "Nice catch."

A stupid catch, I thought to myself. Error, Jake Kratzer. Here I have the program that can control the game, and I nearly lose it chasing a silly baseball.

"You'll have to get Bakanauskas to sign that," Potbelly said.

"Hey, you'll have to get Wade to sign it," Graybeard piped in. "Especially if he keeps up this perfect game."

"None of that," Potbelly warned. "You'll jinx it."

The crowd moaned, and so did Graybeard. "Bakanauskas just struck out swinging. That kid is really in a slump."

I always thought it was a little weird to hear pro ballplayers called "kid," but I didn't say anything. I stuck the ball in my back pocket and marked a backward *K* in Bakanauskas's box.

The PA system sputtered Lamont Garis's name. I was still probably ten people away from the rest room door, and who knew how many more people were waiting inside?

The crowd got going on a "Gar-ISS! Gar-ISS! Gar-ISS!" cheer that had to be led by the Shoppers mascot. The hollering got louder and louder, and finally erupted with a lot of clapping. I looked at Graybeard. He put his index finger in the air to tell me to wait while he listened over the buzz of the crowd.

"Sorry, the batteries are low in this thing. Garis hit a slow roller down the first-base line. The first baseman got it, but the pitcher didn't cover in time. So Garis is aboard with an infield hit."

In my scorecard I marked off a diagonal line between home and first and put a 3 under it for the infield hit.

The PA system announced Hector Hernandez. "Maybe the little guy will draw another walk," said Potbelly as the line moved forward a couple of steps.

From the groan of the crowd, it didn't sound that way. "Didn't mean to hit it, but did," the guy behind me announced. "Check-swing comebacker to the pitcher. Lobbed to first for the out."

1–3, I wrote down. End of the fifth. And now what? I had an important responsibility, but I was

still eight people away from the front door to the
men's room.

			R	H	E
Visitors	000	00	0	0	0
Shoppers	000	00	0	3	0

Top of
the Sixth

"Shoppers fans, it's time for the Apex Exter-
minating pop-fly contest. Remember, Apex can
eliminate flies and most other bugs in one pop.
Our contestant tonight is Ted Healy of Wakena."
There were boos from the crowd. There always
were when somebody rooting for the other team
got picked.

"If our contestant can catch three pop flies in
a row, he'll get the jackpot of two hundred forty
dollars. Ready, Teddy?"

"First popup!" I couldn't see anything from the
men's room line, but I knew what had to be going on. Our first-base coach, Ray Weingartner,
would hit a fungo straight up in the air, and the
contestant would try to catch it in a catcher's mitt.
It wasn't easy. Weingartner could hit fungoes
halfway to the clouds, and if anybody was lucky
or good enough to catch the first two, he'd hit
the third one so high you weren't sure it would
ever come down.

The PA system squawked out a crash and the sound of glass breaking. "Too bad, Ted," said the announcer. "But you do win twenty-five dollars' worth of extermination services from Apex, another fine Shoppers supporter."

That was about what I'd expected. In all the years I had come here, I had only seen one person ever catch the three popups in a row. It was a woman who caught for her softball team.

"Now batting for Wakena, Karasik, right field."

Hey, wait a minute! Hold on! Here the inning was starting, and I was still six people away from getting into the men's room. "Would you hold my place a minute?" I asked Graybeard.

"Sure."

I ducked behind the far corner of the bathroom. It didn't exactly smell wonderful, but nobody was waiting there. So I put my program up against the cement block wall for support and marked a strikeout in Karasik's box for the sixth.

The instant I finished, I remembered what my brother had said about not tiring out the pitcher. But I knew better than to do any erasing.

What I didn't know was what to do about the rest of the inning. I didn't like having strangers watch me as I penciled in what was going to happen next. So I had the idea of filling in the

91

whole inning all at once, right now. The problem was that I had no idea whether it would work.

There was another problem. I really did have to pee. I didn't know if I could hold it in for another inning. I peeked around the corner. The line had grown even longer. If I lost my place, who knew how long I might have to hold it in? Maybe another *four* innings.

And if I didn't put the whole inning in the scorecard now, I might be in the middle of peeing when the next batter came up, or the one after that. So I figured I might as well try it. Quickly I wrote in what I figured would be two popups. Fenneman, to the second baseman: 4. Piccolini, to the shortstop: 6. Then I folded the program over so that nobody could see the scorecard and wandered back into line. From where I was standing, I couldn't see the end of it.

"Almost there," said the guy in front of me.

"One ball, two strikes on Karasik," said the guy behind. A roar went up from the crowd. "Make that strike three!" Well, I expected the first one to work.

The crowd was still so loud that I could barely hear the PA announcer call out Fenneman's name. Potbelly shook his head as he moved through the door. "Man! We're missing . . . well, you know what."

I knew what, all right. A perfect game. I took the baseball out of my pocket and turned it over, just to give myself something to do.

"Ball one, way outside," said the guy behind me a second later. The crowd turned quiet. Big 4, I kept telling myself. Easy pop to second base.

Then I heard the crack of the bat and a worried sound from the crowd. "High fly," said Graybeard, my personal announcer. "Should be an easy out for Shoop in left." The crowd sent up a big round of applause. "He got it."

The ball had gone to left field instead of second base. My idea of prescoring the inning hadn't worked!

I stepped through the door. Three or four more people and I'd be at the urinals. But who cared? Facing Fenneman, for the first time since back when I'd erased that play on Pelc, Dirk Wade had been totally on his own. Now, for Piccolini, he'd be on his own again.

"Ball one," said the guy behind me. "Halfway up the backstop." Oh, boy. Great. Perfect. Wade would lose his control and his perfect game, all because I had made a pig of myself on root beer.

A spot opened up at the urinals. As I stuck the baseball back in my pocket, I wondered what ballplayers did when they had to go to the bathroom in the middle of the game. I mean, you didn't see players calling time and suddenly coming in from right field shouting, "Time out! I've got to go!"

Anyway, I went. The big exhaust fan at the end of the room was so noisy you couldn't even hear the crowd. As I zipped up my fly, I looked around for the guy with the radio. No luck. I washed my hands in a hurry at the big round washstand and waited in line for a paper towel. I ran outside so fast I nearly stepped in a half-eaten tray of nachos somebody had dumped on the ground.

As I worked my way back to the stairs, the crowd was getting pumped up. A little kid with a big cone of cotton candy bumped into me, or maybe I bumped into him. I picked some of the sticky stuff off my shirt and hurried up the stairs. All I wanted to do was see what was happening to Wade. At the top of the stairs a couple of beer vendors were blocking the aisle, watching the game. I squeezed past them and looked out.

Wade glared in at Piccolini and shook off a sign. Wade glared in again and shook off another one. I glanced out at the scoreboard. Three balls, two strikes. Full count. Wade nodded, wrapped his fingers around the ball, wound up. He delivered.

Piccolini put his bat out and sent a little looper out past short. Garis went back, back, back, and stuck his glove up. The ball popped in. And bounced out again.

And then somehow Garis caught it with his bare hand before it hit the ground. He fell on his butt, but he held onto the ball.

The crowd hollered its loudest yet. The buzz just wouldn't stop. Perfect game still standing through six. Time to fix my scorecard.

And then I got this sick feeling in my stomach and my throat and everywhere in the rest of my body at once. My scorecard wasn't there.

		R	H	E
Visitors	000 000	0	0	0
Shoppers	000 00	0	3	0

Bottom of the Sixth

The beer vendors were giving each other high fives at the top of the stairs as I ducked under the trays that dangled from their necks. How could I have been so stupid? I kept asking myself. How could I have lost the scorecard? It had to be the dumbest thing I had ever done in my entire life!

As I went down the stairs, I patted my back pocket. At least the ball was still there. Nice, but forget about getting Wade to sign it for his perfect game unless I could get that scorecard back. The PA announcer was saying something about the lucky program number to win a hundred dollars' worth of baseball cards, including a special set personally autographed by every player in the Cascade League, but I didn't pay attention. What good would a lucky program number do me when my really lucky program was history?

Where did I have it last? I thought about it. The last thing I could remember was writing the top of the sixth into it back behind the bathroom. I started looking there. No luck.

The line for the men's room had grown even longer, and it didn't seem to be moving at all. Apparently all the beer and soda was working its way through people's systems. Starting from the door, I walked along the line and checked to see if maybe I had dropped the program on the ground.

I spotted it instantly. A little way back, the pages of a program were fluttering in the breeze as it lay on the ground about ten people back from the men's room door.

I ran over and picked it up. I opened it to the scorecard pages. It wasn't mine.

It had belonged to somebody who had kept score for a couple of innings, then given up. Whoever that person was, my grandmother would really have been disappointed in him. Or her. I tossed the program in a recycling bin.

If I had dropped my program outside, it was definitely gone now. I made my way up to the door of the men's room and tried to nudge my way in.

"Hey, where do you think you're going?" said a stubby fellow about my father's age.

"I've already used the toilet," I told him. "I left my scorecard in there."

"Great excuse, bud," said a muscular blond kid in front of him.

"I just need to get in there for a second," I said.

"So do the rest of us," said the blond kid. He stood there with his huge arms folded across his chest, almost daring me to push past.

"Let him in," said the man behind him. The big kid slowly moved aside, but he made sure to give me a good bump as I edged past. Baseball is great, but it doesn't make every fan a wonderful human being.

I ignored him. I didn't care about getting shoved. All I cared about was finding the scorecard. There were only four places it could possibly be: near the line inside, near the urinals, near the washstand, or near the exit.

It wasn't anywhere on the floor where the line was waiting. And I could see it wasn't anywhere near the urinals. So I walked around a little partition and looked near the washstands. Right beneath somebody's foot, right where I had been standing, was a program. It had to be mine.

I waited for the foot to move away, then pounced on the program. The outside was kind of soggy, since it had been sitting in a puddle of water that had dripped from the washstand. I opened the program to the scorecard pages.

It wasn't mine. Whoever bought this scorecard

hadn't even bothered to write down the first inning. Both the Apples page and the Shoppers page were totally clean. There wasn't a mark on them.

I could feel my eyes filling up with tears. What an idiot! How could I live with my brother after doing such a stupid thing? How could I live with myself? Angry, I tossed the dumb useless program with its dumb empty scorecard into the wastebasket where people were throwing dumb used paper towels.

And that's when I noticed something weird. Peeking up from beneath the program I had tossed into the trash was another program. I looked closer. I could see three more programs through the wire mesh of the basket. I leaned over the edge. I rummaged through the soggy paper towels and picked all four programs out of the trash. I nearly fell in.

"Trying to get some extra lucky numbers, young fellow?" asked an elderly man drying his hands and waiting for me to come up for air.

I shrugged.

"Good luck," he said as he tossed his soggy towel into the bin.

I had the feeling I'd need that luck. I took the four programs into a corner and opened the first one to the scorecard pages. Not mine.

The outside of the second program was damp. The inside had somebody else's handwriting. Not mine.

The third one felt so soggy it was nearly dripping. The pages were so damp they stuck together. But the stiff scorecard pages in the middle were mostly dry.

And they were mine.

"Where have you been?" my grandmother asked in a worried tone as I sat down next to Randy. Somehow the Shoppers had Faria on second and Mountain on third. I checked the scoreboard. Two outs. And it looked like a new pitcher was warming up on the mound for the Apples. I must have missed all the announcements while I was sorting through the trash.

"Big crowd out there," I said. "Long line at the toilets. What's happening?"

"I suppose you'll want me to lend you my scorebook at the end of the inning," Grandma said.

"Please?" I took the ball out of my pocket. "I'll trade you for a look at this foul ball I caught."

"Oh, sure you caught that!" Randy snorted.

"While I was waiting in the men's room line. Remember that high foul ball Bakanauskas hit?"

"So?"

"This is it."

"Let me see that." Randy grabbed the ball out of my hand.

"Let Grandma see it. That is, if she'll let me see her scorebook."

"Perhaps. Perhaps," she teased.

Gramps leaned over toward me. "Quite a game you're missing."

I looked in toward the plate. Steel was up. Fast ball high from the new pitcher, number 44. Ball one. I opened the program to find out who this pitcher was and check his stats.

"What happened to *that?*" Randy pointed to the program. "Looks like you dropped it in the toilet!"

"Good guess." I wiped it across his leg.

"Get that thing off of me! It looks as though you used it for a mop! There's even a footprint on the back cover!"

Steel took ball two, low. Number 44 was a guy named Henry Dallesandro, who had only pitched fourteen innings all season but had a 4.25 ERA, which was pretty good for this league. I folded the program back to the scorecard pages. I had a lot of catching up to do. "I dropped it, okay?"

"And I told you where."

"Randy, chill out, huh?" There was still a little popcorn in the bottom of the enormous box. I grabbed it and stuffed it in my mouth before Randy could make it disappear.

The new pitcher got one over the plate. Steel popped it up toward shallow right field. "Drop in! Drop in!" Randy hollered. The Apples first baseman, second baseman, and right fielder all homed in on it. I was positive they were all going to crash into each other in a giant collision. At the last second, the second baseman waved frantically to call the others off. He made the play off balance and fell down. Out number three. The crowd let out a big sigh.

"Please let me borrow your scorebook?" I begged Grandma.

"I really shouldn't," she said, and handed it over.

It was pretty simple. Mountain singled to left. Faria doubled to right, but the Apples held Mountain at third. Shoop sent a line drive to short, and Horton popped one to second. That's when the Apples manager brought in Henry Dallesandro to get the last out, which was Steel's bloop to Ruidoso.

I fixed up the top of the sixth inning, too. That one I remembered only too well. I just hoped all the sogginess wasn't going to make the scorecard useless. I handed Grandma's scorebook back to her with a big "Thank you." She handed the ball back to me with a "Thank you" of her own.

"They're saying there's never been a perfect game thrown in the Cascade League," somebody told his neighbor a couple of rows behind me. I turned back to look. It turned out to be a beefy man with a porkpie hat who was listening to the game on the radio.

Well, Dirk Wade and I would just see about that. From now on, it would be nothing but concentration for Dirk and me. Just nine more batters and Dirk Wade would go down in baseball history.

And so, in a way, would I.

		R	H	E
Visitors	000 000	0	0	0
Shoppers	000 000	0	5	0

Top of the Seventh

"Shoppers fans, it's time for Monsieur Gar-BODGE to pass through the stands, courtesy of your friends at Solid Waste Recovery, SWR. Please do the polite thing and pass your gar-BODGE down to the man in the tuxedo and the bright-red bow tie. And please turn to page thirty-two of your Shoppers souvenir program for the SWR ad. If you have number six six three two six, you've won a year's supply of gar-BODGE and recycling bags, courtesy of SWR."

"Now *there's* one you might win," said Randy.

I looked. "Nope." I leaned across Randy to Gramps. "Hey, what was the lucky number last inning? The one for the baseball cards?"

"You think I remember such a thing?" Gramps asked.

"Of course you do." Before he retired, Gramps was an accountant. He always remembered the lucky numbers. At the end of the game you could ask him any one of them, and he could tell you right off the top of his head. He always said it had nothing to do with his being an accountant, since Grandma was an accountant, too, and she never remembered. He called it a parlor trick, just something he liked to do to while away the time. "Well?" I asked.

"Five four nine oh two," he said without batting an eyelash.

I waded through the soggy pages of the program until I found the one with the ad for Kollector's Korner. I stared at the number. "What did you say?"

"Five four nine oh two."

"You've got to be kidding, right?"

"What do you mean?" Gramps said with about as much emotion as when he was bluffing us at poker.

"I mean, you looked in here, right? To make me think I won? It's a joke, right?"

"Oh, come on, Jake."

"Well, then how come five four nine oh two is the number that's in here?"

"Let me see that," Gramps said. I handed him the soggy program. "Well, congratulations! Darned if you haven't won!"

"Come on!" said Randy. "I don't believe it!"

"Wakena second baseman, Reynaldo Ruidoso," mumbled the announcer. For some reason he spoke a lot more clearly when the Shoppers were at bat.

Concentrate, concentrate. I flipped to the scorecard section of my program. The page was so damp, the pencil almost ripped the paper, but I managed to mark down a ground out to third for Ruidoso: 5–3. Then I flipped back to the ad for Kollector's Korner.

"Five four nine oh two?" I asked again. "Are you sure?"

"Dream on," Randy told me. "He's kidding you."

"I wouldn't make you embarrass yourself over something like that," Gramps said. "You won, and that's that. Go down to the customer service desk and see for yourself." Ruidoso took ball one way high.

"I can't believe it! I actually won something! It's totally amazing!"

"So is this game," Grandma said. "Anyhow, congratulations!"

"Where is the customer service desk, anyway?" I asked.

"Twenty miles from here," Randy said.

"Seriously." Big swinging strike one for Ruidoso.

"Seriously. It's around third base, between the sausage stand and the ice-cream stand. You

106

know where I'm talking about? There's kind of like a little table out front?"

"Yeah, I think so." Ball two to Ruidoso.

"When are you going down there?"

"Have to collect before the top of the ninth. End of this inning, I guess."

Randy leaned over and whispered in my ear. "Still working?"

"We'll soon find out," I whispered back, pointing to the scorecard. "I just hope it didn't sog out."

Ruidoso took ball three. "Hang in there, Dirk!" boomed a woman behind me, and, "Stay with him!" and, "No walks, no way!" I just kept thinking "grounder to third, grounder to third, grounder to third," hoping it would help.

The crowd noise rose as Wade kicked the dirt around the mound and stepped on the rubber. He wound and threw. Ruidoso was taking all the way. But the umpire thrust out his right arm and bellowed, "Stee-rike!"

The crowd roared. Ruidoso dug in. Wade delivered. Ball four.

Except it wasn't ball four. The ball hit Ruidoso's bat and dribbled down toward third. Bakanauskas bore down on it, picked it up bare-handed, and nailed Ruidoso at first by two steps. The crowd couldn't believe it.

But I could. The scorecard and I were back in business! Not to mention the fact that I had just won a hundred dollars' worth of baseball cards and I had a foul ball in my back pocket. Yes! All right!

Ben Covington stepped up, dug in, swung the bat. Concentrate, I told myself, concentrate. Don't think about all those baseball cards till the end of the inning. Worry about the game. I marked Covington down for a fly out to center field: *8*.

Wade reared back and threw a strike down the heart of the plate. Covington sent the ball high in the air. In center field, Mack Lenihan took two steps, stopped, and snared it.

"Fred Pelc, first base," mumbled the announcer. I thought maybe it'd make Wade feel stronger if he got another strikeout, so that's what I put down.

Wade threw one in the dirt, but Pelc swung at it anyway. "Man, he missed that by eighty feet!" said my brother, peeking at my scorecard.

Wade blew a fast ball right by the batter. "Stee-rike!" the umpire shouted.

"Three pitches, three strikes," Randy predicted. But the next one was low and away.

The pitch after that was a high fast ball. Pelc

thought it was a ball. The umpire thought it was a strike.

Three up, three down. Perfect through seven. As Wade did his little dance across the foul line, I thought I could see him smile.

"I'm going for my prize," I told Randy. "I'm out of here."

"I never thought I'd say this to you, Jake," Randy said into my ear as the PA system played the introduction to "Take Me Out to the Ball Game," "but if you don't get back here in time for the top of the eighth, I am personally going to massacre you."

			R	H	E
Visitors	000 000	0	0	0	0
Shoppers	000 000		0	5	0

Bottom of the Seventh

"Fans, please rise and sing along," the announcer urged. I got up, and I did sort of sing along as I headed back toward the exit tunnel and the stairs. It was slow going, though. The aisles were packed. It seemed as if every person in the place had decided to pick that moment to run out and pee or get a hot dog or a soda or a beer.

"Perfect game," somebody said behind me. "We've got to get back before the top of the inning."

"Hot dogs!" shouted a vendor in front of me. "Don't get caught in those horrible lines downstairs! Buy 'em right here! Hot dogs! Right here, no waiting! Hot dogs!"

"Beer! . . . Beer! . . . Beer!" hollered a frog-voiced vendor up in the stands. Some vendors mixed it up a little — "Cold beer! Ice-cold beer! Beer here!" or whatever — but this guy was ab-

solutely the same every night. Just a deep "Beer!"
and then a long pause. And "Beer!" one more
time. My brother and I once counted forty-two
"Beer!"'s before he finally made a sale.

"You want 'em, we got 'em! Peanuts!" chanted
a vendor in a singsong voice. "You know it, you
want 'em! Peanuts!"

The crowd in the aisle seemed to be going in
both directions at once, and not very fast either
way. I finally reached the stairs, but the crush
didn't ease up until I got to the bottom. By the
time I got there, I heard the PA system sputter
Lenihan's name.

I'd never seen the place so packed, except
maybe last year when they had the San Fernando
Rooster. He's a guy who wears a goofy rooster
suit and runs around making fun of the players,
the umpires, and sometimes even the fans. I liked
him a whole lot when I was a little kid, but I had
kind of outgrown him.

There were lines outside most of the concession stands — except for the sausage stand. The
sausage stand was closed up. It had a hand-
lettered cardboard sign that read RAN OUT OF
FOOD. SEE YOU NEXT YEAR! except NEXT YEAR was
crossed out, and somebody had written in AT THE
PLAYOFFS! The customer service booth was not

next door where Randy said it was supposed to be. And from the sound of the crowd, I figured Lenihan had made an out.

One way or another, Lenihan's at bat was over. "For your Shoppers, third baseman, Tim Bakanauskas!"

I spotted the customer service window a little farther toward third. I kept my eyes and ears open as I went over there. Who knew? Maybe Bakanauskas would hit another foul in my direction.

But he didn't. From the crowd's groans, he had to have made out number two. This inning was moving too darned fast. Only one more out to go, but I still had to pick up my prize and get back to the game.

A skinny guy with a blond moustache, a Shoppers cap, and a badge that read BLAIR was standing at the customer service window. He looked a little older than my brother, and he looked kind of bored. "Yes?" he said as I walked up and the PA system announced Lamont Garis.

I folded my program to the page with the Kollector's Korner ad on it. "I think I've got the lucky number for the sixth inning. For the baseball cards?"

"You *think* you've got it? You either do or you don't."

"Well, I do."

"Let's see."

I handed him the program. It was still kind of soggy.

"Yuck!" He made a face. "What did you do, pick this out of the garbage?"

"It doesn't say the program has to be in perfect condition."

"Perfect? You're lucky this one's still in one piece." He checked the number in my program against a piece of yellow paper with the winning numbers on it. "You're just lucky, period. Yeah, you won."

I couldn't help smiling. Until now I wasn't absolutely positive my grandfather had remembered the number right, even though he always did. In the back of my mind I was thinking maybe Randy had put him up to playing a trick on me. And I found it hard to believe that my "guaranteed lucky" program really had that kind of luck in it.

Now I knew it was for real. There's something about winning that makes you feel good.

The applause from the crowd made me feel good, too. Garis must have gotten on base somehow. The PA system announced Hernandez.

"Here you go." Blair handed me a certificate the size of a dollar bill that said it was redeemable

113

at Kollector's Korner and listed all the stuff they had announced at the beginning of the sixth inning. Then he took my scorecard and put it on a shelf behind him.

"Wait a second!" I protested.

"Wait for what?"

"How am I going to keep score the rest of the game?"

"Who cares?"

"I care."

"You just won a hundred dollars' worth of baseball cards, and you care whether you finish keeping score?"

"It's a perfect game so far. That program could be a valuable souvenir."

"In that condition? Kid, that's not exactly mint."

"It'll dry out."

"It'll all stick together."

"Come on! Give it back!" I was almost shrieking.

"That's not how it works. You get the prize, I get the program."

"That's not fair. What if I win another prize?"

"Fat chance."

"*Some* chance."

"Look, I have to keep the program to prove to

my boss that I gave the prize to the right person. I'm just doing my job."

There was a huge roar from the crowd, and it just kept going. It wasn't fair: Something incredibly exciting was going on out there on the field, and I was stuck here fighting to get my scorecard back.

"Here!" I threw the certificate back across the counter. "Keep the dumb old prize! Give me back my scorecard!"

And then, who should come up behind Blair but the guy who had sold me the program, scratching his beard. I wondered how much he knew about what was going on. "Trouble?" he said to Blair, and then he spotted me. "Hey, didn't I tell you this one was lucky? Guaranteed?"

"You weren't kidding!"

"I never kid about luck."

"You didn't tell me about the other part."

"What other part?"

"How it was going to let me help Wade win the game."

"Huh?"

"You know." I thought he knew. He had to know.

But he just shrugged and shook his head.

115

"Anyway, congratulations." He turned to Blair. "So what's the problem?"

"This kid won a prize, but he doesn't want me to keep his program."

"Hey, I don't blame him. We've got a perfect game going. Give him back the program."

Blair took it off the shelf. "What about the lucky number?"

"Here." The vendor grabbed the program and leaned toward me. "Kollector's Korner, right?"

"Right," I said.

He flipped to the page with the lucky number on it and ripped it right out of the program. I couldn't believe it. I felt as though he were ripping out part of my heart. "Here. Sorry about the inconvenience. Enjoy those baseball cards. And the game. And next time, believe me when I talk about luck!"

I didn't know what to say, but I didn't have time to argue. As he handed the program and the certificate back to me, the crowd sent up a loud roar. But I felt sick again. When I watched that man rip the page out of the program, I was sure he had ripped up my chances — and Wade's — for a perfect game. I guessed he really didn't know.

One more time the roar of the crowd turned into a disappointed groan. It was exactly the way

I felt. And I didn't even know what had happened.

		R	H	E
Visitors	000 000 0	0	0	0
Shoppers	000 000 ?	?	?	?

Top of the Eighth

"Shoppers fans, tonight's paid attendance: seven thousand five hundred forty-two — a new Nottingham Shoppers record. The Shoppers thank you for attending."

The crowd was still pretty thick. I made my way back to our seats just as Ollie Raspberry strode up to the plate. I sat down and gave him a fly out to left field: 7. But I almost didn't expect it to work.

"What did you win?" Randy asked. "I mean, exactly?"

I showed him the certificate. He looked impressed. "Nice going."

"What happened last inning?" I asked. Wade's first pitch to Raspberry was high and outside.

"Nothing much. A couple of pop fouls, a walk. Then Garis stole second, and the catcher threw the ball away and he got to third. Hernandez drew another walk. And Mountain Man, Man Mountain, my guy, belted one to right. Unfortunately, their guy caught it on the warning track."

"Grandma, can I see your scorecard again?" I asked.

My grandmother made a face.

"It wasn't my fault that I won a prize and it took so long to get through the crowd."

"Okay, okay," she said. "But wait till the end of the inning."

"Can't I see it now? I'm way behind."

"Nope," Grandma said firmly. "Wade may be working on a perfect game, but so am I."

"Not a single mistake so far," Gramps said proudly. "I think she may just do it this time."

I didn't want to mess up Grandma's scorecard. I figured I could wait till the end of the inning. Wade delivered high, ball two. Steel tossed the ball back with a little extra "get it down" snap.

Wade wound and threw. Raspberry sent a ground ball up the middle. Garis came over from out of nowhere, gloved the ball, and fired off balance to first. He beat the batter by a step. 6–3. And what a 6–3! Except . . .

"That's not what you wrote down!" Randy whispered to me. "You had him down for a fly out to left."

"I know," I mumbled as I erased the 7. "I know. The guy who gave me the prize ripped

119

out the page with the lucky number on it. They stole my luck!"

"It's not fair!" Randy blurted out.

"What's not fair?" Grandma wondered.

"Oh, nothing. Nothing." Randy leaned over to me. "What are you going to do now?"

"I don't know. I think Wade's on his own from here on out."

"You're not even going to try?"

"Why bother? The scorecard's had it. It's dead. It doesn't work!"

Wade looked in at Gruber. Fast ball across the outside of the plate. Strike one.

"How can you be sure it won't work anymore?" Randy wanted to know. Slider inside. Strike two.

"Oh, I'm sure, all right. All you had to do was see the way that guy ripped out the page." Called strike three!

As I put down the *K*, the crowd whooped and hollered and hollered and whooped some more. In fact, as Bret Klunder stepped in, everybody in the stadium somehow understood it was time to stand up and roar. I stood up with them and did a little roaring of my own. And a lot of hoping.

Wade threw a fast ball. Klunder swung. And missed.

Wade threw a slider. Klunder swung again. And missed.

The crowd was going crazy now. As Wade went into his windup, seven thousand five hundred forty-two people (except for some of the Apples fans, and I'm not sure they weren't rooting for him, too) got loud, louder, and louder than that.

Wade wound. He threw a change-up. Klunder fouled it high down the first-base line.

Faria waited under it and squeezed his glove. The crowd went crazy. The perfect game was still on the books with just one inning left.

Or more, if we didn't get some runs real soon.

And as Dirk Wade walked into the dugout, I could have sworn he looked straight into my eyes and mouthed the words, "Where were you? What happened?"

			R	H	E
Visitors	000 000	00	0	0	0
Shoppers	000 000	0	?	?	?

Bottom of the Eighth

"Shoppers fans, please turn to page thirty-four of your scorecard program. If you have the words 'More Flavor, More Fun' written in yellow on the Nottingham Creamery advertisement, you've won fifty ice-cream cones and ten banana splits. Better bring a friend! That's Nottingham Creamery: More flavor, more fun."

I checked page 34 and made the thumbs-down sign.

"Hey, what do you expect, man? You've got a baseball, a whole mess of baseball cards, and one inning short of a perfect game," Randy said. "You want ice cream, too?"

But I didn't care about that. What I really cared about was the look Wade had given me. What was it all about? I wondered, as Grandma handed her scorebook over to me. What was Wade trying to tell me? Was he in on this somehow?

I turned to the inside front cover with his soggy

autograph. Somehow he seemed to be winking at me from the team picture. Maybe it meant something; maybe it was just all the water the cover had absorbed.

I kept thinking about it as I penciled in the Shoppers seventh: Lenihan, foul out to first: *3F*. Bakanauskas, foul out to third: *5F*. Garis, walk: *W*. Then stolen base, *SB*, and *E2* to get him to third. Hernandez, walk: *W*. Mountain, fly out to right: *9*.

I thought about everything that had happened in the game so far, especially the way the score-card had been working. I made a mental list of exactly what I knew:

1. The minute I erased something, nothing else I did worked for the rest of that inning.

2. If I made anything at all happen in the top of the inning, I couldn't make anything happen in the bottom.

3. I couldn't make anything happen in advance. I had to wait until the batter actually came up to the plate.

Aha! Maybe it worked the other way! Maybe the scorecard wouldn't work as long as it wasn't caught up. So as Tony Faria came up to the plate, what I was thinking was that maybe, just maybe, the problem wasn't that the program had its page ripped out. Maybe, just maybe, the problem was that the scorecard wasn't up-to-date last inning.

But now it was. So if all those rules were true, that meant maybe, just maybe, just a squeaky little maybe, I could so something now. I hadn't erased anything. I hadn't had any effect in the top of the eighth. So as Faria dug in, I gave him a double to right. If it worked, I figured I'd have Shoop pound a two-run dinger and maybe Horton could hit one out too.

Fast ball low from Dallesandro. Ball one.

Sinker low, fouled into the dirt around home plate. Strike one.

And then Faria got around on an inside fast ball and ripped it up the gap in right field. The crowd rose to its feet, and Randy kept screaming, "Go! Go! Go!" But the third-base coach signaled for Faria to stop at second. A good thing, too. Karasik's throw would've beaten him to third by twenty feet.

Nobody out. Man on second. I smiled proudly. I was right. I knew it. I had the magic back again, at least for this half inning. And as I was thinking about what to do for Shoop, the shortstop snuck in behind Faria, the pitcher whirled, and Faria was picked off second.

Nobody could believe it. It was the same play they had pulled on Hernandez when Faria was up in the third. Faria wasn't even that far off base, but he was leaning the wrong way, and the pitcher knew it. It was a play the Apples must have been working on all year. And what a time to use it!

I was kind of in shock as Shoop stepped back in at the plate, and Dallesandro didn't waste any time. On the first pitch, Shoop bounced a high hopper toward second. The shortstop bobbled it and threw down to first a couple of steps too late. As the crowd went wild, I put down a line from home to first and an *E6* underneath.

And then I looked at the scoreboard. The official scorer had given Shoop a hit. "I don't believe it!" Randy wailed.

"Me, neither," I piped in. "I was sure that was an error."

"Error on the official scorer is what it looks like," Gramps said.

But the only official error was mine. Now I had two choices. If I erased the *E* now, I absolutely wouldn't have a chance of getting the magic back for the rest of the inning. If I didn't erase it, the scorecard wouldn't really be up to date. Either way, the magic would be over until next inning.

I decided to leave the error in. But just in case I was wrong about the rules, I put down a home run to left for Dexter Horton.

Horton swung at the same pitch Shoop got, and he did about the same thing with it. Except this time the Apples shortstop came up with the ball and flipped it to second. The second baseman jumped away from Shoop's slide and gunned the ball to first. Double play. End of inning.

Well, I didn't think it would work, and guess what: It didn't. I changed the error to a hit and the home run to a double play. Then I flipped the scorecard over and got ready to concentrate harder than I ever had before.

		R	H	E
Visitors	000 000 00	0	0	1
Shoppers	000 000 00	0	7	0

126

Top of
the Ninth

"Shoppers fans, it's time to check your tickets for the great auto giveaway. In the next two minutes, the fine pre-owned Cadillac that's circling the field could be yours, courtesy of Nottingham Motors. That's Nottingham Motors, for service, selection, and value. Our winner is in section three . . . row seventeen . . . seat eight."

We heard somebody scream way back in the stands behind home plate. Two ushers went up there to get a tall woman with long dark hair who kept squealing and jumping up and down. They took her out onto the field and asked her name and what she thought about her prize. She said her name was Belita something, and she thought the big old car with the enormous tail fins was just fantastic.

"Get moving, get moving," Randy muttered.

"Let's give Belita and Nottingham Motors a

big hand!" said the announcer. They got a small one. Then she got in the car and one of the ushers drove her off toward a door in right field.

"And now she misses the only perfect game in Cascade League history," I said.

"Maybe, maybe," Randy muttered, then shouted, "Play ball!"

"What do you mean, maybe?" I asked. "We've got it in the bag. Right here." I pointed to the scorecard.

"What if he freezes up?" Randy said.

"What do you mean, freezes up?"

"You know, like in a rain delay. With all this stuff about the car, he's been sitting around for a while. And it's getting cooler out."

"It hasn't been all that long. The last inning went by pretty fast. I'm sure he had his warm-up jacket on. And there's this." I tapped the scorecard again.

And then, as Wade strode out to the mound and went into his rosin bag routine, we joined the rest of the fans in a standing ovation. It was amazing. Everybody in the park was hollering and whistling and applauding.

Wade gave himself a good talking-to and patted himself on the butt. He gave a little nod to the crowd. I watched him carefully, but he didn't look at me. He just went to work.

Nobody sat down. I didn't think the yelling could get louder, but it did.

Wade's first three warmup pitches landed in the dirt. "Don't say I didn't call it," Randy muttered.

"You didn't call it," I said. The next pitch looked fine. The ones after that looked even better. Wade gave the ump his deepest bow yet.

"What do you think?" Randy said.

I showed him my scorecard. It already had a big backward-*K* swinging strikeout in the ninth-inning box for Dave Karasik. There was just one problem. "Batting for Karasik, number six, Mark Swindell!"

I groaned. I'd never thought of that. You can always count on baseball for surprises. "They're loading up righties against him!"

"What did you expect? Nobody's hit him so far."

Quickly I penciled Swindell's name above Karasik's on my scorecard. I made a mark to the left of the ninth-inning box to show that a new hitter was up. At least I didn't have to erase anything. But would my stuff work on a pinch hitter, par-

ticularly when I had written it in before he was
even announced?

Well, it didn't break any of the rules I knew
about. I hadn't erased anything. It was the start
of a new inning. And now the scorecard was up
to date. But this magic stuff was weird. We'd just
have to see.

Swindell looked big and dumb and slow.
And powerful. Everybody was still standing
as he took the first pitch for strike one. "All
right!" Fists went up in the crowd, the noise got
louder, and nobody even thought about sitting
down.

Wade looked in, set, and threw. In the dirt.
Ball one.

There was almost total silence as Wade wound
up this time. Swindell took a big cut and sent a
screaming liner down the third-base line.

Foul.

The crowd relaxed a little as the umpire threw
Wade a new ball. Wade wound and threw a slow
curve. Swindell swung way out in front of it. His
foul hit the top of the Apples dugout.

The next pitch was ball two, up and away.
Steel tossed it back with another "keep it low"
gesture.

Wade kicked the dirt around and stepped on

the rubber. Randy pointed to my scorecard. "We'll feel the breeze," he said as Wade delivered the ball.

Swindell's bat stirred up the air, all right. And that was all it got. Steel grabbed strike three and sent it down to first for an around-the-infield trip back to the pitcher.

One out. But I had the feeling that maybe I'd been lucky. Maybe Swindell had struck out in spite of what I'd written down, not because of it. This time I planned on waiting until the batter got announced and stood up at the plate before I picked up my pencil.

But this time there was no pinch hitter. Fenneman, the Apples designated hitter, came up to the plate in his regular turn. *K* time again, according to my scorecard, but this time I wouldn't even give the batter the final swing.

"Good go," Randy said.

"No argument from me."

Fenneman took a big cut at the first pitch. Strike one. Wade threw a breaking ball. It caught the outside corner for called strike two.

The fans were whistling and yelling and stomping again. Just about everybody in the park wanted to see Wade get this guy.

And Wade sent a slow change-up down the

131

outside of the plate. It was such a weird-looking pitch that Fenneman didn't even take the bat off his shoulder.

The umpire punched him out. Randy and I gave each other high and low fives. The crowd went crazy.

Nobody sat down. The noise got even louder. Even Grandma and Gramps were screaming at the top of their lungs. I heard the PA announcer say something, but I couldn't hear what. He must have been announcing the pinch hitter, because the starter, Piccolini, was short and white, but the batter was tall and skinny and black.

"Turn around!" I shouted into the wall of noise. "Show us your number!" But he didn't. The pinch hitter was right-handed, of course, and the back of his uniform was pointed directly away from us.

"What's the call?" Randy said. "Another K?"

"I can't put it in," I told him. "Not till I see his number and figure out who he is."

"In the majors the scoreboard would tell you."

"Well, this isn't the majors." I turned to my grandfather. "Can I borrow your binoculars a second?"

He handed them over as the mystery batter dug in. I put them around my neck and focused on him. No luck. The batter had the kind of straight-up-and-down stance and tight swing that didn't let you see his back even for a second. "I can't believe this guy!"

Wade reared back and threw. Mr. Mystery took the pitch, low and away. The guy was so cool he barely took the bat off his shoulder. "Come on, come on," I muttered.

Wade shook off a sign, then gave that little nod to the catcher. He wound. He threw. And this time the batter swung far enough for me to see that his number was 27. But now it was too late to matter.

Number 27, whoever he was, had hit a looper to center field. Lenihan was charging in, Garis was backing out, and even Apples fans were roaring at them to make the play. Garis veered off as Lenihan dived, skidded a couple of feet along the field, reached out, and reached up.

A mound of white stuck out of his glove like vanilla ice cream on top of a cone. 8! Out number three! Perfect game!

"They won't call him 'Jerk' anymore!" Randy hollered in my ear.

Halfway to second base, Number 27 tipped his helmet to Dirk Wade. The pitcher bowed to him and then to the crowd.

I had nothing to do with the play, but I felt like taking a bow myself.

			R	H	E
Visitors	000 000 000		0	0	1
Shoppers	000 000 00		0	7	0

Bottom of
the Ninth

I don't know how the noise got louder, but it did. Wade tipped his hat to the crowd as he walked to the dugout, and people screamed, "Per-FECT! Per-FECT! Per-FECT!" over and over. When he finally disappeared, the crowd chanted "Wade! Wade! Wade!" He popped out and tipped his hat again. The "Per-FECT!" chant returned.

There was one small problem. The game wasn't over yet. Unless we scored a run somehow, it would be time for extra innings.

"Harvey Haddix," Gramps muttered grimly as the crowd sat down.

"Hope not," Grandma said as if she knew exactly what he was talking about.

"What exactly is a Harvey Haddock? Some kind of cartoon fish?" Randy asked an instant before I was going to. But while I listened to him and my grandparents with one ear, I was trying to listen to the PA announcer with my other ear and check out what was happening on the field. Wakena was making defensive changes, including another new pitcher. I wanted to make sure I got everything down right. If I couldn't stay up to date, the magic would be gone.

"Harvey Haddix," said my grandfather, "was a pitcher for the Pittsburgh Pirates. In one game against the Braves in 1959 — and this was the Milwaukee Braves, before they moved to Atlanta — "

" — and after they moved from Boston," Grandma piped in, "which even I am too young to remember — "

" — he pitched twelve perfect innings. Twelve perfect innings in one game. Thirty-six consecutive batters retired. Nobody did it before, and nobody's done it since."

"Impressive!" Randy admitted.

"He lost the game," Gramps said.

"He *lost* the game?" Randy asked.

"How could he lose the game?" I wondered.

"His team didn't get him any runs," Grandma said.

"Twelve singles, but not one run," Gramps added.

"And in the bottom of the thirteenth inning, the Pirates third baseman misplayed a ground ball," Grandma said.

"Don Hoak." Gramps shook his head. "He threw low to first. That put Felix Mantilla aboard."

"The perfect game was gone. But at least it was still a no-hitter," Grandma pointed out.

"The next batter was Eddie Mathews, and he sacrificed," Gramps said. "Mantilla on second, but still a no-hitter. And you'll never guess who came up next."

"Babe Ruth," Randy joked.

"Close," Grandma said. "Henry Aaron, actually."

"You're making this up," Randy insisted.

"You can look it up when we get home," Gramps told him.

"Anyway, they were not about to let Henry Aaron hit," Grandma said. "So they walked him intentionally. Runners on first and second."

"Didn't matter, right?" I pointed out. "Bottom of the thirteenth? Only the lead runner would count."

"That's what the manager thought, too. Still a no-hitter, by the way. And up stepped another pretty good hitter, fellow by the name of Joe Adcock," Gramps said.

"Now here comes the interesting part," Grandma informed us.

"I remember this exactly," Gramps went on.

137

"Adcock hit a home run over the center-field fence."

"Unbelievable! You *are* making this up," Randy said.

"It got crazier yet. Aaron thought the ball had hit the fence, and since his run wouldn't count, he cut across the diamond after he touched second. But Adcock kept running, and when he touched third, the umps called Aaron out for being passed on the bases. Anyway, it didn't matter, because Mantilla had scored. But under the rules, Adcock's homer officially became a double."

"So for Haddix, it was a thirteen-inning loss, one to nothing," Grandma summed up. "And his game went into the record books as a one-hitter."

"Geez," Randy and I said almost at the same time.

"So this game is not exactly over yet, is it?" Gramps asked.

"I'll say it isn't," Grandma said.

I got the scorecard straightened out just as Steel stepped up to the plate. Swindell replaced Karasik in right. Mystery man, number 27, turned out to be a guy named Dobbs Smith, but he was out of the game. Number 15, Orestes Agostino, replaced Piccolini at short.

The new pitcher was a righty, Scott Hofmeister. From the warmups he seemed to have a hard fast ball and a slow curve. And I had nothing to do but watch.

"Steel! Man of Steel! Hit one out!" cried my brother. He took the first pitch, wide.

"Good eye!" we both shouted, and, "Tater time!" Steel lifted one down the first-base line foul.

"Straighten it out!"

Steel did. He got around on the next pitch for a shot straight to center field. Raspberry caught up with it, but somehow it bounced off his glove and started rolling toward the wall. By the time the right fielder caught up with it, Steel chugged into second. The official scorer ruled it a double.

Lenihan stepped in and took a couple of practice swings as though he would go for the fences. But my grandfather and the Apples knew better. The first baseman charged in for the bunt. Lenihan popped the ball in the air to make things easy. One out. 3 unassisted.

"Be a hero!" I shouted to my man Bakanauskas. I gripped my foul ball for luck. Bakanauskas took two balls, then sent a weak pop to the shortstop. 6. Out number two.

It was all up to Lamont Garis. Garis choked way up on the bat and kind of chopped as much

139

as he swung. The first pitch was outside for ball one. The second pitch was inside, ball two. Garis took the third pitch, but it was right down the middle.

Two and one. Garis made his chopping motion. Steel danced a little way off second. Hofmeister delivered. And Garis sent a high pop foul toward first base. Pelc trotted over and grabbed it.

"And so, Shoppers fans, we go into extra innings," said my brother in his not-very-convincing imitation of a radio announcer.

"Harvey Haddix," muttered my grandfather one more time, shaking his head.

"No way," I said. "No way." Not if my scorecard and I had anything to say about it.

				R	H	E
Visitors	000	000	000	0	0	1
Shoppers	000	000	000	0	8	0

Top of the Tenth

There were no announcements from the PA system this time, just old music I didn't recognize. Nobody had expected the game to go ten innings, so the Shoppers were all out of prizes. Besides, how were they going to top that car? I didn't think they were about to give away an airplane or a house or something. And you could hardly hear the PA system anyway over the roar that greeted Dirk Wade as he took the mound.

I stood up and hollered with the rest of the crowd, and then I looked down at my scorecard: 27 up, 27 down. The top of the Apples lineup was due up again. Reynaldo Ruidoso was in the on-deck circle swinging the bat, but for sure I was going to wait until he came up to the plate before I put down his strikeout. And then I noticed something I had actually noticed before but never bothered to think about much: There were no columns on my scorecard for extra innings.

"What a cheapout!" Randy had said a week ago when the Shoppers won a twelve-inning game against the Big Cedar Elks. What you had to do was either draw new columns in the margins, where there wasn't exactly a lot of room, or else use the columns where you were supposed to put the box score. *AB* would take care of the tenth, and if it went into the eleventh and twelfth, you could use the columns for *R* and *H*. After that there were the margins, and after that you were on your own.

Grandma's scorebook went up to the twelfth. But unlike her, I didn't believe in keeping a running box score while the game was going on. It was too much work to keep track of. Besides, if you went back and toted up the box score after the game, it was sort of like living the game all over again in your head.

Which I admit I hardly ever did, either. I planned to go back someday and tote up all the box scores in my program collection, but exactly when, I had no idea. Except for tonight's game. I expected to be filling in the box score for this one pretty darned soon.

But when I crossed off the letters *AB* and

marked a *10* above them, I had a sinking kind of feeling. I had the feeling that this time I might just be all out of luck. There might not be ten innings of miracles in this scorecard — only nine. I had to try, though. I put Ruidoso down for a strikeout. One more *K?* I wished.

The crowd was on its feet again now, screaming, hollering, hoping for another out from Wade. Ruidoso fouled off two curveballs, then drilled a fast ball up the middle. Right at Wade, out number one. My eraser got busy again.

Randy noticed. "What happened?"

"No tenth inning on this scorecard. I think Wade's on his own now."

"Well, he got the last batter last inning without your help," Randy said. "I bet he's good for a couple more."

Ben Covington came up to the plate. I marked him down for a ground out to short. But he swung at the first pitch and sent a tremendous pop-up out to first base. 3. More erasing. Two pitches, two away. No help from me.

I sighed. It may sound silly, but in a crazy way, I felt relieved. It was almost more exciting not knowing what was going to happen than knowing what was going to happen because I said so. Almost.

Anyway, the pressure was off. I could enjoy the game, instead of just worrying about it. "Any peanuts left, Gramps?"

"How can you think of peanuts at a time like this?" Grandma said.

"Grandma, you're talking about Jacob 'Mr. Beef' Kratzer," Randy reminded her.

Big Fred Pelc stood in.

Pelc took a fast ball for strike one. Then came a curve and a big swing for strike two. Now everybody was chanting "Strike three! Strike three! Strike three!"

But that's not what we got. Pelc sent a screaming line drive down the right-field foul line. "I don't know . . ." Randy said. And then we did know. The umpire was pointing toward fair territory, meaning fair ball. A second later, it dropped in just to the left of the foul line.

"I guess he figured out what to do with a wooden bat," my grandmother said sadly.

"Good-bye, perfect game," I said. "Good-bye, no-hitter."

"Harvey Haddix," Gramps muttered.

Pelc churned for second as Duke Mountain ran toward the ball, but just before he got it, the weirdest thing happened: A kid Randy's age jumped out of the bleachers in right, picked up the ball, and ran off with it.

It was like one of those lowlights films. A few of the people in the stands began laughing. But there was nothing to laugh about.

Mountain couldn't believe it! He threw up his hands, then chased the kid. Holding the ball in the air, the kid ran toward home. A couple of ushers finally caught him just before he got to first base, and Mountain grabbed the ball from his hands.

But Pelc hadn't stopped running. Before Mountain could figure out where to throw, Pelc had crossed the plate. Hands on his hips, Wade stood there watching it all, shaking his head.

The ushers dragged the kid into the dugout. The crowd applauded. But the important action was going on right at home plate, where the umpires were having a conference. Both managers came out to join them. And when the session finally broke up, the umpires motioned to Fred Pelc and sent him to third base.

Hake, our manager, ran back to the umpires and started hollering at them. "Third base?" Randy screamed. "That guy's so slow he probably never hit a triple in his life." The fans agreed. You've never heard so much booing in your life.

I looked it up on my soggy stat sheet. "One triple this year."

"See? What kind of call is that?" Randy demanded.

"Fan interference again," said my grandfather. "The umpires have the right to award the batter the base they think he would have made."

"Pelc wouldn't've run on the Mountain Man."

"Mountain had a long way to go to catch up with that ball. Remember, Pelc hit it to the opposite field. They were playing him to pull."

"I still say, what kind of call is that?" Randy demanded.

"A fair one," Grandma said. "Darn it."

"The game's not over yet," I said. "It's still a shutout."

"A double shutout," Randy pointed out. "So far."

The Shoppers manager went back to the dugout, yelling at the umpires all the way. When the boos died down, Ollie Raspberry stepped up to the plate. Then Wade straddled the mound. The crowd was already standing, and the boos suddenly turned to cheers.

The noise was deafening. It wouldn't quit. Pelc had spoiled the perfect game, and also the no-hitter, after 9 and 2/3 innings, but you could bet that standing on third there even he had to be impressed with Wade. Wade had to tip his cap all around before the crowd would quiet down even a little.

Still a shutout and the division championship on the line. Wade got set, looked over to the runner on third, and delivered. Raspberry rifled a low liner into left field. Pelc strolled home, Raspberry stomped onto first, and the Apples dugout was full of high fives. Wade stood on the mound just shaking his head as if he was mad at himself.

"I can't believe it! I can't believe it! If Pelc's on second instead of third, the run never scores. Fan interference!" Randy screamed. "That's the lamest thing in the world."

"Oh, I don't know," Gramps shot back. "In this game, there may have been a lot more fan interference than we know about." I couldn't prove it, but I had the uncomfortable feeling he was talking about me.

The Shoppers manager went out to the mound. He said something to Wade, and Wade shook his head again. Then the manager patted him on the butt and ran back to the dugout. The crowd cheered for Wade one more time.

And now it was Slade Gruber's turn at bat. He waited out a low curve for ball one. He watched a high fast ball for ball two. He swung at a change-up and sent it bouncing toward first base. In one swift move, Faria fielded it and stepped on the bag.

One run on two hits. The crowd was so quiet you could hear the ghost of Harvey Haddix.

				R	H	E
Visitors	000	000	000 1	1	2	1
Shoppers	000	000	000	0	8	0

Bottom of the Tenth

Scott Hofmeister took the mound again for the Apples. Hector Hernandez was due up. But there was no way our manager wasn't going to put up his biggest guns.

"Now pinch-hitting for your Shoppers, number twenty-one, Rasheed Olembe!" Olembe had been a football and baseball star in college, but now he was just another minor leaguer trying to catch on. He wasn't in the starting lineup tonight because he didn't do much against lefties.

The Apples manager came out of the dugout, pointed to the bullpen, and went out to the mound. Hofmeister handed him the ball and left the game. In came a pudgy little lefty with a big black moustache. "Now pitching for Wakena, number fifty-five, Lou Torchia."

I checked the stats. Torchia had an earned run average of 2.17. I sighed. "Their stopper, I guess."

"Lefty's got a nice fast ball," said my grandfather. "We saw him earlier in the season."

"We're doomed," said Randy.

"It's not over till it's over," my grandmother warned.

"Have you ever heard of a guy named Harvey Haddix?" Randy joked.

Torchia finished his warmup pitches, and Olembe headed back to the dugout.

"The wheels are turning," Randy said. "The wheels are turning."

"Hake's going with a lefty, right?" I asked.

"Hake's going with a lefty, left," Randy answered. "It's not over till it's over."

"Now batting for your Shoppers, number twenty-nine, Ward Bledsoe," said the announcer. Bledsoe had a lot of power, but he struck out a lot, too.

"Get a piece, Ward!" Randy shouted.

"Dinger time!" I hollered.

Torchia wound, threw. Way outside for ball one.

Torchia got the ball back, turned it in his glove, stamped the mound. He wound. He threw. He missed everything but the dirt. Ball two.

The catcher made one of those "calm down" gestures and tossed the ball back. Torchia went back behind the rubber for a second, looked like he was thinking about something, and then got ready to pitch. In the dirt again. Ball three.

You knew Bledsoe was taking all the way now. All Torchia had to do was lob one in right down Broadway. And that's what he did. But he missed, low. Ball four. Bledsoe loped down to first.

Duke Mountain came up to the plate. The crowd got back on its feet again. "Running for Bledsoe, number two, Rafael Colon!"

"Strategy, strategy. They're playing this like a World Series game," my grandfather said excitedly.

"We need an exclamation mark, Colon!" Randy shouted. Sometimes I don't know where he comes up with these things.

Klunder, the catcher, went out to the mound. The infielders went out to the mound. The manager went out to the mound. I could see through the binoculars that Torchia was just listening. The others were doing the talking, and he seemed to be getting an earful.

The umpire strolled out to break up the meeting and get the game moving again. The manager gave Torchia a pat on the butt and trotted off.

Colon danced off first as Duke Mountain stood in. He took ball one high and ball two in the dirt. Ball three was somewhere in another solar system. Colon was all the way down to second before the catcher figured out where the ball had gone.

Klunder decided that maybe he'd better go out to talk to his pitcher again. The first baseman had the same idea. And that's when my brother leaned over to me.

"Home run to left," he said.

"You think so?"

"Write it down."

"It's useless. It doesn't work now."

"Write it down," Randy insisted.

"What's the point?"

"Will you write it down before this guy makes his next pitch?"

"I don't get it."

"You don't have to get it. Just do it."

"Double or nothing?"

"Double or nothing. Okay."

"That includes the popcorn." We shook on it.

So I marked down a whole diamond with a little dot at the bottom, the number 7 in the lower left-hand corner, and *HR* in the middle. Why not? On this scorecard, you wouldn't even begin to notice one more stupid erasure.

The meeting on the mound broke up, and Torchia looked in. "Ball four! Ball four!" the crowd chanted.

"See? He's got to groove one," said my brother.

He did. And the Mountain Man got all of it. You could tell from the way it sounded. It had the home-run sound. It had home-run distance.

And it went foul by two feet. The crowd sounded as though it had been punched in the stomach.

But the crowd managed to get the "Ball four!" chant going again. And this time it worked. The pitch was a lot closer than the other ones, but the umpire called it a ball.

Runners on first and second. "We could win this thing," I said. "We could. We really could. And you owe me four dollars and another box of popcorn."

"I had to try, didn't I?" Randy said. "He's my man. He came close."

So Colon and Mountain danced off second and first, and that brought up Tony Faria. I kept thinking how things would have been different if only I had known back in the first inning what I knew now. If I had given Faria a home run instead of that triple or that double, we would be shutting down the lights and going to the playoffs on the momentum of a perfect game. Now . . . well, three outs to go. It's not over till it's over.

And then, all at once, it *was* over. Faria drilled a rocket to Agostino at shortstop. Agostino stepped on second to catch Colon off base and fired a bullet to nail Mountain one step off first. A triple play!

"I did mention this guy named Harvey Haddix, didn't I?" said my grandfather.

					R	H	E
Visitors	000	000	000	1	1	2	1
Shoppers	000	000	000	0	0	8	0

Post-Game

"Ladies and gentlemen, boys and girls: The Nottingham Shoppers management sincerely thanks you for your support and hopes you'll be on hand for all the great Shoppers action next season. Please take advantage of our post-game specials while they last: Remember, any remaining item on that tasty Shoppers menu can be yours for a mere fifty cents."

"I hope they're not out of popcorn," Randy said, but his voice sounded kind of flat. He must have felt the same way I did. Talk about anything but the game. It was still too fresh and too painful.

"You're buying," I told him. "I hardly got any of that first box."

"Not my fault you had to pee."

The Shoppers mascot had disappeared, but the crowd started chanting anyway. "Wade! Wade! Wade! Wade!"

Every time they yelled the word, they yelled

155

it louder. And finally Dirk Wade poked his head out from the dugout, tipped his cap, and shrugged. The crowd applauded. Wade waved his cap with a final flourish, and disappeared into the dugout. There was one more huge cheer. The noise slowly died down. Fans began filing out of the stands.

No perfect game. No no-hitter. Not even the championship. "Kind of breaks your heart," Gramps muttered.

"No need to hurry," Grandma said. We usually stuck around awhile rather than fight the crowd to get out of the park.

"Did you ever see a triple play before?" I asked them.

"Never!" Grandma said.

"On TV," Gramps told us. "This was the first time in person. What a way to end a game!"

Grandma handed me her scorebook. "Look!"

I looked. It looked a whole lot neater than mine.

"Not even one erasure. Not even one cross-out. It took a perfect game for me to have a perfect game."

"Do you have a great grandmother or what?" Gramps said.

"Nice going," I said. "But for Wade it was only a perfect game through nine."

"Nine and two-thirds," Grandma corrected me.

"Haddix went twelve," Gramps pointed out. "Of course, that was before the designated hitter."

"That scorecard of yours doesn't look too great," Grandma said to me.

"No kidding," I muttered.

We sat there for awhile. A few minutes later, the lights went out around the outfield the way they always did after a game. Eddie Sundstrom, the Great Racer, came out in silver and blue coveralls and began raking the dirt on the mound the way he always did. But there wouldn't be a game here tomorrow. If the Shoppers had won, there would have been.

It all seemed like a dream. But if it was a dream, then how come I had the scorecard and the baseball and the certificate from Kollector's Korner? Or maybe I was dreaming those things, too.

And maybe I was even dreaming about that popcorn. There wasn't any left when we finally went through the tunnel and down the stairs. "You want a fifty-cent hot dog?" Randy asked. "That's all they've got left."

I shook my head. "Kind of lost my appetite."

"I know what you mean," Randy said.

"It's getting late," Grandma pointed out. "Do

157

you guys want to stick around and try to get autographs?"

"We've got the whole weekend to sleep," Randy said.

"Yeah. Especially now that we won't be in the playoffs."

"We came close," Grandma said.

"Close only counts in horseshoes," Randy mumbled.

"Oh, it counts everywhere else, too," Gramps said thoughtfully. "It's not the same as winning, but it counts. We'll meet you guys in the usual place?"

"Right," Randy said as we headed for the area where the players came out.

"You think we'll be able to get Wade's autograph?" I wondered out loud.

"He's gonna be mobbed," Randy said.

"But he sort of knows us," I reminded him.

"That could be good or bad. Maybe he will sign stuff for us because he knows we're fans of his. But maybe he'll sign stuff for other people because he figures it's a first for them. You never know."

"I want him to sign my scorecard," I said.

"That'd be a collector's item, all right," said Randy. "Assuming you can ever get it dried out."

"Don't worry. It's already drying out."

"What about Bakanauskas? You going to get him to sign that ball?"

"I don't know. I think I want Wade to sign it."

"But he didn't throw it. The other pitcher did."

"But it's still a ball from the perfect game."

"The perfect game that wasn't."

I spotted Wade with a mob around him. He finished a couple of interviews for people with microphones and cameras and notebooks. He said he was glad he had such good defense behind him. He said it was too bad he hadn't been able to hold on and get the Shoppers to the playoffs. He said that was baseball. He posed for some people with flash cameras.

And then the rest of the mob started holding out baseball cards and baseballs and mitts and bats and scorecards. Wade patiently signed them one by one.

"I'll bet you're still the only one with his name on a basketball," Randy said. "Or underpants."

"You think I can get him to do both the ball and the scorecard?"

"Who knows if he'll even get to us in the back here?"

And then, after some more signings, Wade stared at me and shouted, "Hey, basketball!"

I didn't get it.

"You," he said, pointing straight at me. "Yeah,

you. You were the one who had me sign that basketball, right?" he asked while he kept on signing other people's stuff. I was glad he didn't seem to remember the underpants.

"Yeah. That was me." I moved in closer.

"So what do you want me to sign this time?"

"My scorecard. And this baseball."

"Glad to do it. Glad to do it."

I handed him the baseball, and he signed it and handed it back. Then I handed him the scorecard. "Could you do it on the Apples page? Because they're the ones you got out?"

"Most of them, anyway." For some reason, he took a little longer to sign that.

"I'm sorry you lost the game."

"Me too. Just another *L*. And no playoffs. But I hear a guy named Harvey Haddix had it worse." He smiled and handed the scorecard back to me.

I thanked him. We walked away.

"So what do you think the scorecard thing was all about?" Randy asked me.

"I don't know," I said honestly. "I have no idea. For a minute there, I thought Wade had something to do with it."

"I have another theory."

"You always have theories."

"Well, maybe you weren't making things happen at all. Maybe you were in some sort of time shift. You know, you sort of knew ahead of time what was going to happen, and that's what you wrote down."

"That's the silliest thing I've ever heard."

"Look up there," my brother said, pointing straight up.

"What?" I didn't see anything but the night sky. "Stars of the past, man," Randy said, smiling. "Stars of the past. Most of that light takes thousands of years to get here. We're looking at light that started out before we were born. Before Grandma and Gramps were born."

"So?"

"So something could happen way out there in space right now and the news wouldn't get here till we were dead. So maybe somehow it worked backward and you got to peek into the future."

Stars of the past. Stars of the future. My head was getting dizzy. "It makes as much sense as anything else," I said.

We caught up with Grandma and Gramps, and the last of the field lights went out. This had happened before, so we were ready for it. We stood in one place while Grandma hunted in her purse for her flashlight. Grandma always came prepared.

She found it and switched it on. "Let's go."

"Can I borrow that for a second?" I asked. "I

just want to see what Wade wrote in my score-card."

Grandma handed the flashlight over to me, and I pointed it at the scorecard. There on the top, right below where it read Visitors, was Dirk Wade's familiar signature. And above it was something else.

I smiled and handed the flashlight back to Grandma.

"What did he write?" she asked.

"Nothing special," I said.

But I was kind of telling a fib. What he actually wrote was pretty special as far I was concerned. What he wrote was, "Thanks, Jake. I couldn't've done it without you."

About the Author

Stephen Manes has written more than thirty books for kids and adults, including *Chocolate-Covered Ants*, *Comedy High*, *The Great Gerbil Roundup*, *Some of the Adventures of Rhode Island Red*, *The Obnoxious Jerks*, and the Hooples and Oscar Noodleman series. Children in five states have voted his best-selling *Be a Perfect Person in Just Three Days!* their favorite book of the year. Its hero, Dr. K. Pinkerton Silverfish, recently returned in the sequel, *Make Four Million Dollars by Next Thursday!*

Mr. Manes covers the computer industry as a columnist for *The New York Times*. He cowrote the best-selling adult biography *Gates*.

Mr. Manes has also written screenplays, software, and place mats. He lives in Seattle, Washington.